THE FIRE WAS SPREADING.

Jessica backed up, took a deep breath, and made her run.

Bullets sang all around her, the tongues of flame licking at her, but she managed it. She hit the rooftop hard, rolled, and dove to reach the wounded sheriff.

Beneath her she could feel the vibrations of someone crossing the roof, and she gestured with two sharp jabs. She would take the one on the left; let the sheriff take the one creeping up from the right.

Jessie waited, her finger wrapped around the trigger of the Colt double-action revolver. Still, when the witch appeared, it was with sudden savagery. She carried no gun, this one. Instead, her hand was wrapped around the handle of a huge bowie knife.

Jessica rolled to one side and kicked out with both boots, sending the witch tumbling head over heels. But as Jessie whirled, coming to one knee, the witch lunged at her again. . . .

WESLEY ELLIS

LONE STAR

AND THE
DEVIL WORSHIPERS

J

JOVE BOOKS, NEW YORK

LONE STAR AND THE DEVIL WORSHIPERS

A Jove Book/published by arrangement with
the author

PRINTING HISTORY
Jove edition/August 1990

For information address: The Berkley Publishing Group,
200 Madison Avenue, New York, New York 10016.

ISBN: 0-515-10386-1

Jove Books are published by The Berkley Publishing Group,
200 Madison Avenue, New York, New York 10016. The name
"JOVE" and the "J" logo are trademarks belonging
to Jove Publications, Inc.

PRINTED IN THE UNITED STATES OF AMERICA

10 9 8 7 6 5 4 3 2 1

Chapter 1

The lady was an assassin. She was a nice-looking, dark-eyed woman wearing black. As the Comstock Central train rolled through Painted Gorge on its way to Fort Collins, Colorado, she found herself sitting across the aisle from a tall, athletic-looking man who might have been an Indian but was in fact Japanese-American. Beside him, sleeping as the train rolled on through the hilly country, was a young, very pretty blonde.

The man's name was Kiai, and along with his companion, Jessica Starbuck, he was riding the rails west to discover why the railroad was having trouble getting timber for its ties. There was no real explanation for it; all that Kiai and Jessica knew was that the Chinese and Welsh laborers had simply walked off the job. Without the ties, the railroad dead-ended halfway to Fort Vasquez, and it was the army post that the railroad, an arm of the far-flung Starbuck empire, was intended to reach. The army wanted beef for their soldiers brought in, and without the railroad, it would have to be driven overland.

Now it looked as if the expense of laying the tracks out of Kansas and purchasing rolling stock was going to be a dead loss to Jessie Starbuck.

The train jerked as it slowed down for the bend that led down from Painted Gorge to Fort Collins, and Jessica Star-

1

buck woke up. She glanced at Ki and through a yawn asked, "How long now?"

"Less than an hour," Kiai answered. His eyes were still on the dark-eyed woman across the aisle. She smiled, fleetingly, and then went back to looking out the window at the rolling countryside.

Jessica yawned again and stretched her arms. The man beside her was one of the best—and deadliest—men in the West. Kiai was her friend, protector, confidant. A master of the martial arts, he was the most gentle man Jessie had ever known—until violence was threatened.

"She's beautiful," Jessica Starbuck said, and Ki slowly turned his head toward her.

"I didn't notice."

"No," Jessica answered, "I could tell."

The gorge rolled past, a beautiful orange and deep-maroon slash in the green Colorado hills. Ahead now Jessica could see the vast expanse of timberland leading up to the great barren peaks of the far mountains. Alex Starbuck, Jessie's father, had once traveled this countryside and bought up miles of land, not for the timber or the ore, but for the sheer beauty of the hills. For a no-nonsense businessman, empire builder and speculator, he had had a touch of the poet in his soul, it seemed.

The train, on the flats now, slowed and rolled on across the grasslands. Already Jessica could see a few outlying ranches, a man at work in the fields. In another fifteen minutes she could make out the low, sprawling outline of the town of Fort Collins.

The train inched its way into the station with the bell clanging and steam gushing. Ki stood to recover his satchel from the rack overhead, and as he did the lady in black lunged at him.

From the corner of his eye, Kiai saw the flash of steel, the

2

sudden movement, and it was enough for him to duck and block the slashing knife with his forearm. Ki reached out to grab the woman's arm, but he was a hair too slow. Black lace ripped from the cuff of the her dress, and she pulled away, running for the door of the still-moving train.

Ki, dropping his satchel, was on her heels, but again he was too slow. He reached the door in time to see the woman in black leap from the train and roll down an embankment. She lay sprawled on the grass for a moment before she got to her feet and, with her skirts hoisted, dashed for the trees beyond.

Ki was still standing on the platform between the Pullman cars when Jessica arrived, followed by an anxious conductor.

"I saw that," the conductor said. "What in hell happened?"

"You know as much as I do," Ki answered. "I've never seen her before today. I'm sure of that."

"She was going for the throat, Ki," Jessica said. "She wanted to kill you."

Ki nodded, "Yes, I know that. It was all planned, too. She took the seat opposite me deliberately. But why?"

He was leaning out, holding onto the rail, but he could catch no sight of the woman in black as the train braked to a squealing stop and, with a final whoosh of steam, invited the passengers to disembark.

It was a hell of a welcoming.

Ki backtracked while Jessica waited at the depot, but there was no sign at all of the woman. "She just took off into the timber and kept going," Ki said with a shrug. "There was a horse waiting for her."

"Miss Starbuck?" the voice from behind them said, and Jessica turned to find standing there a man of five-feet-six with bushy red sideburns. There was a faint expression of trepidation in his eyes.

3

"That's right," Jessie answered.

"I just heard what happened on the train. I'm so sorry. I'm Jules Jenkins, station manager for Comstock here."

That made him one of Jessica Starbuck's employees, which explained a part of the uneasiness. He glanced at Ki, hesitantly stuck out a small hand, which Ki shook, and they were introduced.

"I'd like to talk to you in your office," Jessica told the railroad man.

"Of course. Shall I have your baggage taken to the hotel? I'm sorry to say we have only one hotel for decent people in Fort Collins, but it really is quite nice."

"If you would, I'd appreciate it," Jessica said. The little man still looked nervous, and giving it a second thought, Jessie Starbuck realized why. If the railroad couldn't be completed, Mr. Jules Jenkins would find himself without a job.

They followed the short man to his office, a modest gray and green room across the depot lobby. A stiff, narrow secretary watched them enter, his rigid collar slicing into his neck as he, too, struggled to impress the owner of the Starbuck empire with how industrious and indispensable he was.

"Please sit down, Miss Starbuck," Jenkins said inside his office. "May I get you something to drink, cool lemonade, say?"

"No, thank you." Jessie sat on the edge of a deep red divan, her hands between her knees. "I assume you know why Ki and I have come all this way, Mr. Jenkins."

"Yes, of course." Jenkins frowned and picked up a letter opener, which he kept turning in his pudgy hands. "The construction problems. Unfortunately, I know as little as you do about the cause."

"It's not Indians, is it?" Ki inquired. Jenkins glanced at Ki as if he had forgotten he was there.

"Not to my understanding, no. Oh, it's true there are Utes

4

in the mountains, but if there had been trouble like that, the word would have spread like wildfire. It's almost, Miss Starbuck, as if there's a conspiracy of silence in the timber camp.''

"There's nothing to do but ride up there," Jessica said. "Bob Sachs is still running the show, I suppose."

"Yes, and he's quite all right, only he doesn't come into town anymore. If you want my *opinion*, Miss Starbuck, I think the problem centers around the fact that most of these timbermen are foreigners. The Welsh are all right, I suppose, but always brawling and drinking. And the Chinese," he shrugged, "well everyone knows they're lazy to begin with . . ." Jenkins looked again at Ki, now seeing the oriental cast in his eyes. "I beg your pardon, you're not . . . ?"

"No, I am not Chinese," Ki replied. "Still, in their name I shall take offense."

"It's very illogical beyond all other objections," Jessica said thoughtfully. "No matter how lazy a man might be, still he's got to feed himself and he doesn't come all the way to these far reaches to sit down on a job."

"Well, then," Jenkins muttered ineffectually, "maybe it's some sort of strike. Maybe they're dissatisfied up there in Game Trail."

That had occurred to Jessica, too; in fact it was her initial reaction. But she knew that the lumberjacks and mill workers at Game Trail Camp were being paid well enough by the Starbuck company. If, in fact, they were getting the pay that was coming to them, they were making twice what a cowhand did, and with the free room and board, they should have had no complaints of any sort.

"There is no point in further speculation," Ki said. "All we can do is ride up in the morning. For myself, for this evening, I would like to eat and then suffer a good night's

5

sleep—something a railroad passenger, unfortunately, must forego.''

Jessica was in total agreement. Her own bones ached from trying to sleep in her plush Pullman seat, from the nearly complete lack of exercise. She was on her feet as Ki rose, stifling a yawn. They had started to say good-bye and start for the door before Jenkins said, ''You do know about the army liaison?''

''Pardon me?'' Jessica said. Someone hadn't done his job. This was the first she had heard about it.

''The army,'' Jenkins went on with a rush, ''has dispatched a first lieutenant named Travis to coordinate the investigation. The army, Miss Starbuck, wants that beef taken through to Fort Vasquez as badly as we want the railroad line completed.''

Outside, the railroad people were only now unloading Ki and Jessie's horses, leading the big gray and the paint down a wooden ramp onto the rear of the platform. Jessie slipped the men a few dollars to have the animals stabled up and fed, then she and Ki, enjoying the chance to stretch their legs, walked to the hotel, which had ''Royal Grand'' emblazoned across the face of its false front.

There was a restaurant in the hotel, and Jessie and Kiai went directly to it, sitting in a quiet corner to eat. Then they walked down a smoky corridor to their facing rooms. In Jessica's room, already two girls of fourteen or so were filling up a galvanized bathtub with steaming water poured from two huge pots.

Outside, it was growing dim as dusk crept over the mountains. Jessica said, ''There's no point in trying to do anything much tonight, is there, Ki? I'm ready to fall down into a dead sleep after this bath.''

''I don't know what else can be done,'' Ki answered. ''But

6

I may go out into the saloons and talk to the working men. They may know something their bosses do not."

"Only if you feel like it. For myself," she said around a yawn, "it's bath and a sleep."

Then she lifted a lazy hand in farewell and went into the room, leaving Ki to himself in the corridor.

Ki's own room was silent, musty, dark. The last western light still cast long shadows across the floor and walls, and by that light alone he changed clothes, removing his traveling suit, unpacking his cork-soled sandals, black jeans, blood-red shirt and leather vest.

He patted the vest, assuring himself that his *shuriken*, throwing stars, were in the many pockets of the vest. Then he slipped into it and stood at the window for a moment, enjoying the cool night air.

The first star was blinking on through the haze of twilight, and uptown the lights of the gaming halls, the houses of prostitution, the late eateries were being lit. One by one they went on and little by little Fort Collins transformed itself from a hardworking frontier town to a hard-gambling, hard-drinking night spot.

Cowboys from the outlying ranches drifted into town by twos and threes, laughing as their horses shuffled their way up the main street toward the pleasure palaces at the far end of town.

Respectable women scurried home, trying to escape the oncoming darkness, and the women of the night began to emerge, painted and raucous.

All of this was familiar to Kiai. How many Western towns such as this had he seen, how many had he and Jessica Starbuck traveled through, happy to leave when it was possible? At times Ki longed for the quiet, jasmine-scented nights of long ago, the gardens of the monastery where he was raised, the huge Japanese moon. . . .

He closed the window and, with a slow deep breath, went out into the streets of Fort Collins. It was no time for longing, but a time for working.

Tinkling music drifted from the dance halls and saloons of the frontier town as Ki walked the plank walks, seeing the sullen faces of Welsh miners and squatting Chinese. They stood or sat outside the buildings in groups of nationality, watching the tall man as he studied the town.

Ki tried it: "Any way a man can find work around here?" he asked a dark Welshman, and the man only shook his head and turned away. "I've been a miner, a ranch hand, a lumberjack . . ."

The man just walked away, leaving Ki alone on the dark street corner. A group of three Chinese at the next corner didn't bother to lift their eyes to him as he repeated his question. It was as if the town were a haunted place and the men moving along its streets specters in the night.

Inside the dance halls the cowboys and sodbusters continued to yahoo it up, apparently without a care in the world, but the timbermen were only shadows outside the brightly lighted windows.

The blond woman scurried toward Ki, her head down. An attractive blonde in the black of mourning, she looked eager to be home in her warm house rather than on the streets of Fort Collins. Ki stepped away as she passed him and then suddenly flung himself to one side.

From the reticule she carried, the woman had pulled a small pistol, and the night exploded with sound as a flash of light illuminated the alley mouth where Ki had landed. He rolled to one side as the woman fired again.

By the muzzle flash he could see her face, pretty yet contorted, her eyes wide, mouth twisted savagely. It was a brief picture, a savage and unforgettable one, one set deeply in Ki's mind before there was the sound of boots running toward them up the plank walk. The woman, looking once more in Ki's direction, took to her heels and fled up the street, and Ki, dusting himself off, stood and tried to explain to the crowd of curious citizens that someone had attempted to hold him up.

It was an acceptable lie. One by one the people drifted away, not interested in another armed robbery, a nightly occurrence in the rough frontier town.

In a few minutes only Ki was left behind in the alley. He stood there for a long time, pondering what had happened without reaching any conclusion at all. Another of the ladies in black had come. For the second time that day a young woman he had never seen before had tried to kill him and he hadn't a clue as to why.

He only knew they would try again.

Chapter 2

Jessica Starbuck could only shake her head.

They sat at their breakfast table in the hotel dining room. Ki had just finished his small breakfast of tea and toast as Jessica worked on her ham and eggs. With the unfolding of Ki's story of the previous night's event, Jessica became more confused.

"I thought the woman on the train had made a mistake," she said, "thought you were someone else. Or, secondly, that she was a demented person of some kind. But you don't encounter two demented women who single you out for their target—not in one evening, Ki."

"So what does it mean?"

"It means that someone wants you dead," Jessica said logically, "but why, who, what the cause of it might be, I can't begin to guess, Kiai. We've only just arrived in town."

"Unless it has something to do with the reason we are here, the problems at Game Trail Camp. And that makes no sense."

"No," Jessica said with a slight smile, pushing her plate away from her, pouring another cup of coffee from the pewter pot on the table, "so far as I know we hired no women as lumberjacks up there."

"Then for now it must remain a mystery. Let us do what we have come here to do and perhaps this will come clear."

"Yes . . ." Jessica, now wearing jeans and a man's cotton shirt, her flat-crowned hat hanging behind her on a rawhide string, was thoughtful again. "We've got to get up to Game Trail as soon as possible this morning, find Bob Sachs and figure out what in hell is going on around here . . ."

Her sentence broke off as her eyes lifted to the door of the dining room. The young man there was blond, tall, broad-shouldered, his expression self-assured. He looked directly into Jessica's sea-green eyes from across the room and strode toward them.

"Miss Starbuck?" he asked. At Jessica's nod he said, "Lieutenant Roger Travis out of Fort Vasquez. I was told you and your companion were down here. The army sent me over to try to find out just what is holding up the Comstock Central. We assumed the railroad was on schedule to beat winter. If it isn't completed soon it will be too late to even try to start a trail drive in from Wichita and we'll have a lot of hungry troopers at the post."

"It will be completed," Jessica said positively.

The young officer spoke with a touch of humor in his voice, but his eyes said there was nothing at all funny about the soldiers at Fort Vasquez trying to survive the winter without adequate provisions. Jessica's declaration did little to remove the grimness from his face. She couldn't blame him. She had no idea yet what was wrong, let alone how to remedy it.

Ki's description of the men from the lumber camp sitting idly up and down the streets of Fort Collins was confirmed when the three emerged from the hotel and started walking toward the stable down a side street. Everywhere Jessica looked, men, appearing lost and frustrated, some even frightened, stood or perched on horse rails. It defied explanation.

Travis saddled Jessica's horse for her and slipped the little

11

paint pony its bit as Ki checked his tall gray horse over for any possible travel injuries.

The sun was still low above the wooded hills when the three started out of Collins toward the timber camp in the mountains.

The road to the timber camp was deeply rutted by the passage of heavy lumber-carrying wagons, but as Ki pointed out, no wagons had been up or down the road for a long while.

"If I didn't know better," he said, "I would think that the camp had been abandoned."

"It seems it virtually has," Travis said. The army officer wore mufti: red-checked shirt, jeans, a wide white hat. On his hip was his service revolver.

They topped out a low wooded ridge and found themselves riding through a long grassy valley where wildflowers still bloomed in profusion. A buck mule deer bounded away from the water hole to their right and lost itself in the deep coolness of the woods.

Beyond the meadow was a tiny town—a collection of three buildings, all weathered gray. The store was closed, the smithy open but vacant. The third building was of indeterminate use.

Together the three rode up the street, which was muddy from a spring that apparently had its source directly in the center of the road and sent a rill trickling toward the meadow.

Two small boys emerged from behind a building, took one look at Jessica and sprinted away. Ki heard one of the boys yell out a warning.

"It's one of them! It's one of them, run!"

Jessica, too, had caught the shouted warning. "What in the world was that about? One of *who*?" she asked.

"I have no more idea than you," Ki said. A frown settled

12

on his features as they continued to ride. Perhaps, after all, he *did* know.

The timber grew taller and deeper now, blue spruce and jack pine with cedar scattered among them and, in the pocket valleys higher up, aspen, beginning to turn.

The lone rider heading toward them on muleback was in his sixties, wore his white hair long and carried an old Sharps repeating rifle across the saddlebows. He squinted into the morning sun as he neared Jessica and her companions and finally halted his mule, removing his flop hat to wipe back his thinning hair.

When Ki and Jessica reined up beside him, Lieutenant Travis just behind, the old man spoke.

"You know where you're headin', young people?"

"To the timber camp," Jessica said. "Game Trail Camp. It's not far ahead, is it?"

"It's not far ahead," the old man said. "But I asked, do you know where you're headed?"

If it was some sort of riddle, Jessica had no answer to it. Perhaps the old man was hard of hearing. She simply repeated what she had said.

"Yes, to the timber camp. I'm the owner. Why?"

Ki asked, "It seems you are trying to tell us something, sir, will you explain what your meaning is?"

The old man shook his head. "It ain't my business; you'll find out. Wander them mountains long enough and you'll find out. That's why I'm leaving."

Then he heeled his jenny mule and started on past them, leaving Ki, Jessica and Travis to stare after him.

Travis circled a finger around his temple. "He's crazy. Happens to a lot of men alone in the mountains too long."

Ki wasn't so sure the man was crazy, but he didn't respond to Travis. He just started his horse on, following Jessica as

13

they traveled the road toward Game Trail Camp, moving deeper into high timber country.

The camp, when it did appear, was a collection of workers' shacks scattered across a nearly denuded slope with, below these, an office and company store. Farther upstream along the shallow, wide creek, was the mill itself, from where the sounds of a buzzsaw could be heard.

There was also the sound of axes, and here and there they saw men moving among the trees, but these were very few. The hundreds of lumbermen Jessica Starbuck had hired to work the timber were absent, the remaining handful of men lethargic and, as Ki noticed immediately, carrying weapons.

Bob Sachs wasn't hard to find. The red-bearded, scowling foreman sat in his office, arms folded, staring at the door as it opened and the three walked in. The room was cold— Sachs wore a mackinaw—and across the floor was sawdust and bootprints. On the wall hung a two-man saw and an old Kentucky long rifle. In one corner a small desk sat unused with ledger books scattered over it. In the opposite corner stood a small green safe with gold scrollwork.

Sachs watched them warily, almost antagonistically, for a moment before his expression changed, his eyes reflecting recognition, and he rose from his chair.

"Miss Starbuck?" he asked.

"That's right." She shook Sachs's hand, an act which seemed to surprise him, and introduced Ki and Lieutenant Roger Travis.

"Sit down," Sachs said, and now his face was almost relieved. Brief puzzlement clouded his features as he realized he only had two chairs besides his own, but when Ki chose to stand and lean against the wall, that moment of bafflement passed and Sachs returned to the chair behind his scarred desk.

"I didn't expect you to come yourself," the timber boss

14

said to Jessica. "Maybe it's best that you did. I haven't gotten anywhere at all with this problem. In fact just before you walked in, I was considering writing up a letter of resignation. I'm not doing my job, and I don't take pay for a job I haven't done."

It was Travis who said, "If you don't mind me asking, Sachs, why exactly haven't you been able to do your job? Why have these men walked out?"

"They're superstitious, sir," Sachs said. "The Welsh are a superstitious race and so are the Chinese. I've done my best, but they can't be whipped, coerced, hired to work up in these mountains anymore."

Ki glanced at Jessica. The vagueness of Sachs's reply had struck both of them. Ki tried to clarify matters: "They are superstitious and so they've quit the job."

"That is correct, sir," Sachs said, "and there's nothing I can do to stop them from walking. Of course once people start to get killed . . . who can really blame them?"

"You've had men killed?" Jessica asked. "I'd heard nothing about that."

"It began after I wrote you. We have a few men left working out here, as you see, but they're thinning out too. Yes, Miss Starbuck, I lost three men last week."

"Lost them . . ."

"To assassins."

Jessica still couldn't figure out what Sachs was working around without saying. He seemed embarrassed, as if whatever he said would not be accepted as truth.

Finally she asked him flat out, "What are they afraid of, Sachs? And who is killing our people off?"

Sachs bit at his thumb and then sighed deeply, "Why, it's the witches, Miss Starbuck, it's the mountain witches that are doing it all."

Jessica couldn't even respond. Ki just frowned deeply.

Travis laughed out loud and Sachs looked from one of them to the other.

"I knew you wouldn't believe me. I know it sounds ridiculous, but that's the situation up here, and it's one I'm not equipped to handle. That's why I was thinking of submitting a letter of resignation. I can run a timber camp, Miss Starbuck, I can keep books, repair broken mill equipment, and if necessary I can whip a man into shape, but this . . . I can't deal with it at all, and I've let you down."

Jessie's voice was quiet but forceful, "Are you telling us seriously that the workers believe in witches?"

"There are witches in these mountains," Sachs said gravely. "My people are afraid of them. The Indians are leery of them. Strange things go on up here, things to make a grown man tremble. And now, with the murders and all."

"This is absurd," Lieutenant Travis said. The blond officer was choking back another laugh. "Do you mean to tell me that my troopers at Fort Vasquez are looking forward to a winter of starvation because a bunch of superstitious lumberjacks are afraid of a coven of witches? Witches, my friend, have not been believed in for centuries."

"They should be then," Sachs said. His eyes were totally serious. "For they are real, sir, and there are many of them in these mountains."

Travis started to reply, but Ki cut him off with his own question, "Have you seen any of them, Sachs?" Ki's question was serious, for he found it hard to believe, looking at the big-shouldered, red-bearded man, that he was afraid of gremlins and specters, spooks or witches.

Hesitantly Sachs formed an answer. "I believe . . . yes, I have seen them, sir. On two occasions."

Travis laughed again and started to rush on with his mockery, but again Ki spoke first. "Can you tell me how they dress, Mr. Sachs?" Jessica's head came up abruptly. If Travis

16

was puzzled as to where the questions were leading, she no longer was. Sachs answered the *te* master's question.

"They dress in black, sir. Always in black."

"Ki!" Jessica said and Kiai nodded. He, too, had seen witches, if indeed that was what they were or pretended to be. He had seen his first on the train and his second on a dark street of Fort Collins, and he fully believed that they were capable of murdering lumberjacks, for they had already tried twice to kill Kiai himself.

Outside stacked thunderheads were beginning to build in the northwest above the towering peaks, and the land was going gray and silent.

Jessica put her hat on and adjusted the string on it as Ki looked toward the deep woods. Travis, crouched against the earth, drew idly with a short stick.

"What now?" the army officer asked. "This is absurd. We supposedly know what has run the laborers off, but how do we fight their superstition?"

"We don't," Jessica Starbuck said, turning toward him. "We fight the witches. That's all there is to do. Whoever they are, whatever they are, it is the witches that must be stopped. And so," the honey-blonde said, "we will find them, and we will stop them."

Chapter 3

Fort Collins sat draped in a cold curtain of rain. The lights from uptown barely reached through the screen of grayness to the hotel where Jessie, Ki and Travis sat at the restaurant discussing the day's events and trying to plan a course of action. There seemed to be no reasonable way to attack the bizarre enemy Sachs had described.

"The local law won't be any help," Travis said. "There's a town sheriff and his deputy, but he won't go into the mountains to chase a bunch of might-be witches around the hills. He says he has too much to do just trying to keep Collins safe for decent people."

"The army . . ." Jessica began and the blond officer laughed.

"Yes, I can see me wiring Major Gordon that I need a company of men down here, that the whole problem is a bunch of witches flitting over the mountains, scaring workers off. It would probably be the end of my own career. No," he said, "there's no help coming from that quarter."

"Then," Ki said logically, "it is up to us—the three of us. Our first task must be to find where these people are located. There could not be that many places to live that far up. Nor could so many people possibly hide out forever."

"The Indians?" Jessica suggested.

18

"Perhaps, if they would talk to us. It's worth a try. Anything is worth a try at this point, Jessie."

"When the storm lets up," she answered. "In the meanwhile we have to try to get some of the lumbermen to talk. If they haven't been working then they undoubtedly need money. Maybe a little gold will conquer their fear."

"We can try it," Ki agreed. "There's little else we can do until the storm clears. I do not like this, Jessica," he said in a different tone of voice. "Either we have some people up in the mountains who are using superstition to close down the timber camp for their own purposes . . . or we are dealing with more dangerous people, those who really do believe in black magic, who are willing to kill for Satan and believe themselves invulnerable."

"I prefer to believe it is the former," the still-skeptical Travis said.

"So do I," Kiai said honestly. "So do I, for they would be far, far less dangerous."

"You really believe that, don't you?" Travis said.

"Yes," Ki answered. "There is little more dangerous than a fanatic. It does not matter so much what these people are as what they *believe* they are."

Travis remained behind to finish his coffee and take care of the bill as Jessica and Ki walked through the dark lobby of the hotel toward their rooms.

"What do you think of him, Ki?" the green-eyed blonde asked.

"Think of Travis? Is he competent, do you mean?"

"I meant, do you like him?" she said, and it was suddenly obvious to Ki that Jessica did like the young officer, and so he gave her the answer she wanted.

"Yes, I like him," Kiai said, and Jessica squeezed his arm briefly, smiling brightly.

In her room Jessica opened her traveling bag and from a

19

concealed compartment removed a leather pouch that contained twenty gold double-eagles. It might or might not work, but it seemed to Ki that if he were an out-of-work miner he would be willing to sell his soul let alone a little information to acquire twenty dollars in gold to feed himself and his family.

Jessica made him promise. "Ki, do be careful. I know they've already tried to kill you twice . . . and I know how difficult it would be for you to hurt a woman if you were attacked."

Ki's answer was grim as he tucked the double-eagles away. "I will be as careful as possible. As for harming a woman, I do not wish it as you say; but I would prefer taking the life of an assassin of either sex to losing my own."

Then Ki said good-bye and moved out onto the porch of the hotel, watching the rain drip from the eaves of the awning, the constant downpour across Fort Collins, the occasional slash of lightning against the dark, rolling sky.

He started uptown again through the darkness and wind, the rain and thunder. It was, he considered, a fine night for witches.

Lieutenant Roger Travis made his way to Jessica Starbuck's room and rapped twice on the door. When she opened it she was smiling, beautiful. The light from the lamp on the wall behind her haloed her light, freshly brushed hair.

"I just came up to see what you and Kiai wanted me to do tonight. I figured I'd poke around myself and see if I can come up with any information."

"It couldn't hurt," Jessica answered, and then she stepped back into the room, leading him by the hand. "Maybe you should give it a try . . . later."

The rain still fell, the lightning still arced across the dark skies above Fort Collins. The bed behind Jessica Starbuck was wide and inviting.

Travis heeled the door shut behind him and pulled Jessica to him, kissing her mouth deeply. Her eyes shone as she responded, her hands going around his waist and onto his slim hips.

"Just a minute," she said, pulling away. Her fingers moved down along the line of buttons on her shirt, and she unfastened them a little slowly, teasingly as Travis, his body answering her invitation, watched.

Jessica removed her shirt and stood, her full, tantalizing breasts bare now before Travis, who felt his mouth going dry, his pulse increasing its rate. He kissed her again, tangling his fingers in her honey-blond hair, and let his hands roam to her breasts, his thumbs running over her taut pink nipples.

Jessica laughed and stepped away. Sitting on the edge of the bed, she removed her boots and then stood to step out of her jeans, revealing long, sleek thighs and the intriguing patch of curly hair between them.

Throwing off the bedspread, she fell back onto the bed to lounge, her head propped up by one hand, watching Travis.

"You're not coming to bed with your clothes on, are you?" Jessica Starbuck asked.

"No," the army officer said, "I don't think so."

He was out of his shirt and boots in a minute, flinging his clothes to the corner of the room. Jessica beckoned to him, and he stepped to the bed, where she unbuckled his belt slowly, caressing the growing bulge beneath his pants as she did so.

Travis felt the heavy throbbing in his groin grow more insistent. There was a slight trembling in his legs as the beautiful young woman unbuttoned his trousers and let them fall to the floor.

Her hands encircled the rigid manhood she had revealed, and slowly she kissed him, one hand hooking behind Travis to clench his hard buttocks.

21

Then she rolled back on the bed and, gesturing with one finger, summoned him after her. Travis crawled onto the bed and kissed her mouth deeply as his hands roamed breasts and thighs and touched the warm dampness between her legs.

Jessica kissed his ears and neck, clinging to him briefly before she rolled onto her belly, rising to hands and knees. Travis moved up behind her, his hands on her beautiful, smooth ass as Jessica reached back between her legs to find him and position him.

Three strokes put Travis in to the hilt, and Jessica sighed with pleasure, putting her head down on the pillow, her hair fanning out, half-hiding her face.

"You don't have to wait," she murmured and Travis didn't. His body began to tremble as he moved against her, penetrating deeply as Jessica continued to make small pleasure sounds in her throat. He could feel her body respond, grow damper and softer as she reached back to touch him and feel the driving hardness of his body where he entered her.

Travis arched his back and, holding her by her thighs, yanked her against his body time after time until he could hold back no longer and came with a violent shaking of his body.

Slowly he sagged over her, his hand reaching in front of Jessica to cup her breast, and together they collapsed into a deep, much-needed sleep, Jessica still smiling as the lantern on the wall burned out.

Ki wandered the rain-darkened town, having little luck in his pursuit of information. No one, it seemed, would speak of the witches. The Chinese huddled together in the shadows of the awnings and stared with silent eyes at Kiai, and not even offering them gold did a thing to loosen their reticence.

Up the street still the saloons roared and shrieked and rang with cacophonous sound. Ki pushed through the green batwing doors of the first one he came to, moving out of the sweep of wind and rain into the smoky warmth of the Silver Dollar.

There men perched on chairs surrounding poker tables or crowded around the roulette wheel or stood in a long, grim line along the scarred walnut bar. A girl in red satin got up wearily and moved toward Kiai, fixed smile in place on her rouged lips, but Ki waved her away.

He was not a drinking man, but he moved up to the bar to stand between two men in worn flannel shirts and order a whisky. With one of the double-eagles he paid for the drink that stayed untouched before him on the bar. The man on Ki's right—big, burly, white-bearded—eyed the change Ki received from a bored, thin bartender.

"Times being good to you, are they?" the bearded man asked finally, looking at his own empty glass and then at Ki's stack of silver dollars.

His voice was slow, grainy, tinged with a Welsh accent. Ki asked him, "Can I buy you a drink?"

"I'd be grateful. Things haven't been going real good for me."

Ki lifted a finger, and when the bartender caught the gesture, he poured the white-bearded man a drink. Kiai said, "You must be working up at the timber camp."

The man's eyes clouded over with brief suspicion. "Why do you say that?"

"It seems," Ki answered, "that nine out of ten men in town do. I've been told they've closed down the operation up there."

"Closed it down," the lumberjack said as he downed his straight whisky, "or been closed down—it's all in how you look at it, my friend."

"What do you mean?" Ki asked. The man was looking

23

wistfully at his empty glass, and so Ki bought him another shot of the raw whisky.

The lumberjack was silent for a time, turning his glass on the bar, meditating on something—the whisky or his answer to Ki. Finally he replied.

"It's a terrible place, the lumber camp," the Welshman said. "I don't think you'd believe it or understand it if I told you."

"Perhaps not," Ki said, "but I'm interested."

The lumberjack's watery eyes searched Ki's face for a long minute. Then he downed the drink in a gulp and turned, back against the bar, to stare at the saloon crowd.

"I'm a working man. I want to work. I've been known to have a drink, but I've never been like this . . ." The Welshman's voice faded out, although Ki did hear him murmur, "So far to come from home—for this."

"Will you have another?" Ki asked, but the lumberman shook his head. Then Ki tried, "Will you let me help you out a little?" and slipped a gold double-eagle onto the bar in front of the man, who eyed Ki suspiciously.

"Who are you? What do you want of me?"

"Nothing," Kiai answered with a shrug. "I am only interested in a good story when I hear one. Yours intrigues me."

"Does it now?" the man asked with a harsh laugh. "If you heard the whole thing, my friend, you'd be more than interested. If you'd have been there, you'd be more than concerned. I'm a strong man, sir, but it still haunts me."

The lumberjack on Ki's other side stared at the white-bearded Welshman and shook his head slightly. Ki's new acquaintance bellowed at him drunkenly.

"I'm tired of keeping quiet about it, McPherson! Damn you, damn all of you—and *them*."

"You'll talk yourself into trouble, Grange."

24

"What more trouble can I get into? What more can they do to me?" the man named Grange shouted again. Then his voice quieted and he said to Ki almost in an undertone, "Come with me, then, and I'll show you a story, my friend."

He swept the gold twenty-dollar piece off the counter and pocketed it, then with a challenging look at the other jack, he tilted his head toward the door and started that way, Ki following in his bootsteps.

Outside the rain had begun to slow. Here and there patches of clear, star-filled, cold sky showed behind the ragged broken clouds. Ki followed Grange silently down the street, tramping across the muddy road into an unlighted alley where a cat scuttled away at their approach.

Ki remained alert. He believed Grange to be honest, a worried but decent man, but one never knew, and Ki had not survived so long in a dangerous profession, in a violent land, by being too trusting.

Grange, walking with the rolling gait of a half-drunk man, moved on steadily through the mud, past the cold, dripping eaves toward a tiny shack that sat behind the stable. There a dim light beamed softly through the oiled-paper window. Inside the shack Ki could hear a low, unidentifiable keening sound.

Grange moved to the door of the small cabin and tugged the latchstring. He pushed the door open and stepped aside, letting Ki enter the dark, musty interior of the shack first.

The room Ki found himself in was cold, very cold. The candle burning on the mantel did little to relieve the blanketing darkness. There was a smoky odor, not given off by the candle, and a deeper, unhealthy scent. A large braided rag rug covered part of the wooden floor; a musket hung over the mantlepiece, an Indian blanket on one wall.

In a corner chair sat the witch.

Chapter 4

Ki glanced at Grange, who had begun to tremble as if from the cold. It wasn't the cold, however, that had weakened his knees. It was silent rage. Ki himself felt an eerie sensation creeping up his spine to the base of his skull as he studied the woman in black.

She sat hunched in a roughly made rocking chair, gloved hands clenched together, her black skirt falling to the floor. Her head was up and she seemed to be returning Ki's gaze, but there was nothing in her eyes, nothing at all.

Grange moved nearer and shifted the candle so that its poor light illuminated the woman's face a little better. She was still young. Her dark hair hung in tangled strands around her shoulders and across her flat breasts. She was as rigid as a wooden figure, an effigy of a woman.

The candle revealed the scars.

The knife had cut deeply and often. Crisscrossing wounds, healed but fresh, ran across her face from ear to ear, across the forehead, from eye to chin.

"You see," Grange said. He spoke almost breathlessly, but Ki could still sense the violent anger in the man. In two sharp movements the lumberman yanked the gloves from the unprotesting girl's hands. Ki winced when he saw what they had covered.

The fingers were gnarled, the entire hand surface wrinkled

and apparently aged. It was not, however, age that had done this, but fire. Ki had seen enough burns in his time to know that the woman had been badly burned and the skin so damaged that it would never regenerate.

"*They* did that to her, my friend," Grange said. "Now do you have an idea of what is happening in these mountains? Do you know who this is, this old, scarred hag?" the lumberman demanded. "She is my wife and she is twenty years old!"

Then he sagged to his knees, the candle falling on the floor to gutter and roll, and as Ki picked it up, Grange buried his face in his wife's lap, sobbing deeply as the woman remained sitting, staring straight ahead without emotion of any description on her ravaged face.

"They did it," Grange said without moving his head. "To teach me, to teach all of us what would happen next, they made her one of them, and then they tortured her because I would go to work every morning no matter what, come hell, high water, hurricane or firestorm.

"No, I don't go anymore, my friend. Now I sit and watch my wife wither and feel myself die a little more . . ." His voice faded and then came back with a roar. "Get out of here! I don't know why I brought you here in the first place. Get the hell out of here!"

There was nothing Ki could do but replace the candle and turn and walk from the shack, leaving the grieving Grange with his scarred and mindless wife.

Grange could have talked on, perhaps, but the silent agony his wife endured told Ki much more. In the mountains, evil walked and the workers hired by the railroad had been far more than superstitious—they had been wise, wise enough to walk away from the darkness of the witches.

It was no wonder none of them had been willing to speak of the coven. Who among them would have wanted his wife, his child to endure what Grange's wife seemed to have endured? Gold could loosen few lips when the price to be paid was much more than a few dollars could ever compensate a grieving lumberjack for.

Ki walked the dark streets of Fort Collins once again. The rain still fell, lighter now, and the wind had increased so that the night grew colder as the gusting breezes carried the chill from the snowcapped mountain peaks down into the long valley.

When they fell upon him, it was as sudden as a bolt of lightning.

They came at Ki out of the darkness. He never knew how many of them there were. A heavy blow landed on his skull as someone tried to club him down with a length of wood. Ki fought back with automatic intensity, side-kicking whoever it was below the heart, driving his attacker back and into the wall of the neighboring building. A barrel toppled over and someone shouted loudly.

The second man took a *nakadate* punch from Ki's trained hands, a middle-knuckle blow that drove the wind from him and sent him reeling.

A gun flashed in the night, red flame blazing close beside Ki's head as he threw himself to the ground. He landed on his back in the mud, but he had presence of mind enough to fish a *shuriken*, a throwing star, from his vest and send it singing through the alley darkness toward his target. The blades caught flesh, and his assailant howled with pain.

Ki heard the attacker's cry but hadn't even the time to see where he had driven steel against meat and bone. Another assassin was leaping toward him as he lay on his back, and Ki lifted his feet, coiled his legs and hurled the man over his head, the attacker's own impetus sending him flying into a pile of trash.

Ki sprang to his feet and assumed the dragon stance, his

28

body poised, his mind alert, but the alley was suddenly empty, his attackers fleeing into the night. Turning slowly, Ki saw an ally he hadn't expected. Grange was behind him, double-barreled shotgun in his hands. He walked to Ki, his face grim, his hair blowing in the cold wind.

"They'll have you," Grange said. He touched Kiai's shoulder and repeated, "They'll have you my friend—believe me, I know. It was them."

Then Grange stooped and from the ground picked up a dark piece of material. It was a veil, a woman's black veil. Grange pressed it into Ki's hand and said very softly, "Be gone, my friend, gone from this country. I know what I am speaking of."

The lumberjack turned and walked slowly, heavily away, toward the small, dark cabin where his woman waited in her rocking chair. Ki wasn't sure just then which of them he felt sorrier for. He himself took a deep breath, looked briefly to the skies, where still a star or two broke through the long, moon-silvered veils of cloud, and slowly began trudging homeward.

Jessica sat up at Ki's knock and covered Travis's sleeping form with the bedspread. Grabbing her robe she slipped into it and walked to the door to find Ki in the hallway. He was muddy and bruised, but otherwise appeared sound. She stepped out into the hallway, her expression concerned.

"What is it?" she asked.

Ki nodded toward his own room and led Jessica into it. Lighting the lantern there, he paced the room slowly, telling her the story as she sat on the only chair.

"The witches."

"This is an evil thing, Jessica. I do not know what has begun it or where it will end. I do not know yet if it is someone's intention to destroy us or if we have merely stumbled into this. But," Ki said grimly, "I shall find out, and we shall end this—whatever its cause or intention."

"Were they women who attacked you tonight, Ki?" Jessica asked.

"At least some of them. One at least was a man. It was too dark to see, but there's no mistaking a man's cry."

"The important thing," Jessica said, pacing the room herself now, "is to locate these people."

"Yes, I agree. And there must be many who know where they are. The trouble is no one will talk. They are afraid of retribution. The Utes, I think, Jessica. Let us talk to the Indians and see what they know. A proper guide and interpreter . . ."

"Travis knows them," Jessica said. "We had some time to talk tonight while you were out."

"Very well," Ki answered with a half-smile. "Then the three of us must talk to them."

"And if we find the witches, Ki . . . ?" Jessica asked, hesitating slightly. "What then can we do?"

"Then," Ki answered, "we will decide. All I know, Jessica, is that until these people are eliminated the railroad cannot be completed. And, as long as these people exist in the mountains, no one else is safe. I have seen what they can do, Jessica. I have seen it and it is an ugly sight."

It was Roger Travis who objected to talking to the Utes. "The Indians aren't going to be any more open about this than the timbermen, Ki," he said when they told him of their ideas. "If anything, they're more superstitious, and more closemouthed than the jacks."

Jessica answered, "It seems, if they are having trouble with these particular whites in the mountains, they might be eager to talk so that something can be done. If they make a move themselves, Roger, it might be construed as an act of war."

30

Still Travis had doubts. He stood looking out the hotel window at the dark skies over Collins, the slanting rain, the subdued colors of dawn over Colorado, and shook his head.

"All right," he said finally. "If you two think it's the way to go. I'm not sure what the army would want me to do. All I do know is that my commanding officer said to get it *done*. It's best not to let them know I'm army if we can do it."

"You know," Ki said as an afterthought, "in the end we may just have to have army forces come in here. The local law's no good, and it may be too much for the three of us to handle."

Travis laughed. "A bunch of women pretending to be witches?"

Ki answered, "You do not know these people or what they have done. Think about it, Travis. They have killed, they have mutilated, they have disrupted the lives of half a hundred men. They have managed to shut down the operations of the Comstock Central Railroad. And I know for a fact that some of their numbers are trained in the martial arts and skilled with weapons.

"I do not know how many of them there may be, but I know that to dismiss them as a bunch of misguided women would be the greatest mistake we can make. I repeat: in the end, we may need the help of the army."

Travis, for all of his fighting experience, all of his years on the plains and in the Western mountains, had never seen the bizarre and violent times Jessie and Ki had, and he was obviously still doubtful. However, he looked at Jessica, seeing the set of her face, and again at Ki, noting the sincerity in the *te* master's eyes, and he shrugged acceptance.

"All right. I'll send a wire today, advising Vasquez that it may be necessary to send a patrol down here. What the colonel is going to make of the wire, I couldn't say. Likely I'll lose my commission."

31

With daylight beginning to brighten the skies, Travis, troubled still, went off to the telegraph office at the railroad station to send his message to his superior officer. Jessica downed three cups of coffee, Ki his usual single cup of tea, and the two of them set out for the stable where their horses stood waiting in dank near-darkness.

The hostler, sleepy-eyed, hung-over and wobbly, saddled their ponies while they waited for Travis to return. When the young army officer did arrive, appearing more troubled than ever, they swung aboard and rode out through the soft early morning rain toward the mountains hidden in the haze of the dwindling storm.

"I thought taking a patrol out against Cheyenne renegades was trouble," Travis said to Jessica as they rode side by side through the pine forest. "At least then I knew what was going to happen, what I was dealing with . . . with this, who knows? A coven of witches in the Colorado mountains—and I'm trying to convince Vasquez that it's real."

"It's real enough," Jessica said, leaning over to rest her hand briefly on his thigh. "You know that."

"Yes, but I may as well have reported that I'd found ghosts lurking here and that was why the railroad wasn't going to be able to get beef through to the fort before winter."

"We *will* solve it," Jessica said, and her eyes reflected that conviction. How it would be done she couldn't have said, but she felt confident that it would be. She and Ki had been through so much, and together they had always found a way before.

She was more sure that the problem could be solved than Kiai was at that moment. As they rode through the tall timber, the cold raindrops dripping from the boughs of the cedar and pine, the jays chattering among the upper branches, Ki held doubts.

He had seen what the others had not seen—a woman

32

slashed and battered by these people. And now he led Jessica Starbuck into the mountains where this had happened. What if something should happen to her?

The master of the martial arts had no fear for his personal safety, but he considered Jessica. She knew enough *te*— open-handed fighting—to defend herself against most men; and she was better with a gun than most of them. But these people frankly scared Ki.

There were only the three of them, and they knew not what they were riding toward or how to prepare for it. When the wind blew it seemed to chill Ki more than normally, and when it shrieked through the trees, the sound the wind made seemed more than natural.

"There are three major Ute camps in the area," Travis, who had done his research, said. "There's a settlement of a hundred or so lodges near the Golden Creek beyond the notch you can see in the hills ahead. Their chief is a man called Nataka. He used to be very warlike, but he's mellowed as he's aged and as the numbers of whites has increased. It's the camp nearest to the timber company, so I suggest we try him first."

"If they are still here," Jessica answered. Winter was coming in hard and many Indians would be moving south by now, following the sun and the buffalo herds. Nataka she had not heard of, but she had encountered the mountain Utes before, as a friend, and as a hostage. She could only hope that Lieutenant Travis's intelligence concerning the man and the Golden Creek Utes was correct and that the white witches haunting the mountains hadn't turned the man bitter, defensive and warlike once again.

It was another two hours' hard ride before they topped a wooded ridge and below them saw the camp of the Utes. Their lodges were scattered among the pines along the river, which ran gray, frothing, swollen with the rainfall. They could see smoke from their campfires, see dogs and children running through the camp, women at work along the river.

And all too soon they saw Nataka himself.

They were all aware of the watchers in the woods, and as they rode down the long slope toward the cold river, Indians closed the trail behind them. Dark-eyed, buckskinned, their hands wrapped around the weapons they carried, they walked behind the three whites as Jessie, Ki and Travis reached the flatlands and aimed their ponies toward the Ute camp.

Dogs ran yapping toward them, children darted in all directions. Nursing squaws and old men stared silently at the incoming riders, and from a yellow-painted tepee, the chief of the Golden Creek Utes himself appeared, shirtless, a silver necklace with a sunburst medallion dangling from it decorating his broad, copper-colored chest.

"Why do you ride this way?" Nataka asked angrily even before the three intruders had reined up and swung down from their horses' backs. "Go on your way. We have no use for you in this camp."

The number of Indians behind Jessie and Ki had swollen to more than two dozen, and now from out of their lodges other warriors appeared. There were no signs of greeting, only the cold, suspicious stares of the Utes.

It was Ki who answered, his first few words in the Ute tongue.

"We wish you only peace, brother. The great chief of the Utes honors us by appearing before us. All we want is to speak to you and any of your people who might know something of some terrible women who haunt the mountains and make trouble for all, whites and Indians alike."

Nataka's scowl continued to contort his face. He studied Ki carefully and slowly answered, "What do we know of the doings of white people?"

"It seems you know something, Nataka. I read it in your eyes. Will you speak to us, if only briefly?"

Nataka turned the request slowly in his mind and finally nodded. "If only for a minute. Then be on your way. There is too much trouble already from the whites."

Ki swung down from his saddle, Travis and Jessica following. Nataka had turned to enter his lodge again without waiting for them.

Inside it was cool, dark, smoky. A silent older woman sat in one corner stitching beads onto a new white elkskin shirt. A tiny fire burned in the center of the lodge. Around it were spread blankets, and at Nataka's curt gesture they seated themselves on these.

Nataka lit a long-stemmed pipe and tossed a burning brand back into the fire. It was some time before he spoke again.

"What is it now that you want? I know nothing of the white women you speak of."

"But you do," Ki said. "All we wish, Nataka, is to know where they are and what mischief they have been up to. We are here to stop them, my friends and I."

"To stop them," Nataka repeated as if he hadn't understood the words.

"Yes, if they are the evildoers we have heard they are, then they must be stopped. I know that the Utes are strong enough to have done this, but you have held back because they are white."

"You are a wise man," Nataka answered. "That is how it has been, yes. There are crazy people in the mountains just now. Now there are terrible people who do strange and deadly things. They are white."

"They are called witches," Ki interjected.

"Witches?" Nataka shrugged. "If you say that is the word, then it is so. I only know that they are bad. Let me tell you some of what they have done," the Ute chief went on. "On

35

some of our hunting trails, dogs have been found hanging by their necks, their paws cut off, their bodies tortured. A child of three is missing; perhaps they did not do this, but it seems they took it. Many nights we hear strange songs like death cries. These people build great fires and dance around them naked. It is unclean, the things they do. Once a young warrior from our tribe saw them with a woman, torturing her. These are terrible people, my friend. Our children must stay in the camp now. Our women are protected. We wish them gone.''

"Where is their camp, Nataka?'' Jessica asked.

"Near the beaver run. On the shallow creek where the mountains split. You would name it Cannon Meadow.''

"Are they there now?'' Ki asked.

"They are there. They are always there,'' Nataka replied. "But be wary if you travel that way, for they have no thought of Manitou or of the Dark Road, no fear of your white gods or of law. They have killed. They will kill again and care not.''

Chapter 5

Ki was strangely subdued as they rode from the camp of Nataka. It was he alone, apparently, who realized that they weren't dealing with a harmless sect of deluded females but a dangerous breed of women specializing in mayhem and death.

He had seen Grange's wife. He had fought with the women—and strong and capable fighters they were. It was true that Nataka's words seemed to have shaken Jessica a little and worried Travis, but still they seemed to ride into the high mountains as if nothing ahead of them could do them terrible harm.

If so, Ki did not share the feeling.

The cold wind seemed more chill, stronger as they reached the creek Nataka had described and pointed their horses toward the split peak ahead of them. Once Ki saw a dark figure, perhaps that of a woman flitting through the woods, but he made no comment and tried no pursuit.

They were in the woods though, and they were watching.

When the three of them found the witches' camp, it was nothing like any of them had expected.

It was deserted, quiet along the river where red-stone bluffs rose up from the slow-running creek. Above them, carved into the stone by nature or by human hands, were caves in three tiers.

"What could bring women out to a place like this?" Jessica wondered aloud. "What can they be thinking of to live in such a place?"

"I wonder more where they are now," Travis said. He had swung down from his horse to study the ground where the tracks of small bootprints, women's tracks, were thick.

Ki sat, his horse still, staring up at the cave mouths. Nothing stirred but the natural elements. The wind whistled through the trees and echoed through the caves; the river whispered past. A red-tailed hawk cried out as it swooped low searching for and missing some small prey.

Jessica, too, swung out of the saddle and stood, hands on hips, hat tilted back, studying the empty camp. Where they had stopped, the banks of the river, topped with stunted cedar, withdrew slightly, leaving half an acre of empty red-sand beach. There, bonfires had been lit, huge blazing things judging from the amount of ash and half-burned log scattered about the beach. In the center of the clearing stood a pole, and around it was scorched rope.

Ki walked nearer and shook his head, not liking the feel of the place at all.

"The pole . . ." Jessica said, and Ki looked at her distantly.

"We can only speculate," Ki replied, but in the deepest recesses of his heart he knew what the pole had been used for, why the ropes had been tied around it. Human torture was not outside of his experience, and he knew too well how brutal human beings could be. But he, too, wondered what went on in the minds of these young women so that they had allowed themselves to become participants in this horrible spectacle.

In his mind's eye, Ki could see the witches swirling around the burning pole as a screaming victim watched them through the sheets of fire. He had no wish to reconstruct the scene

38

or guess what might have happened to what was left of the victims.

"There has to be someone in those caves," Travis said. "Or at least some sign of them."

"We can look," Jessica said. Her hand was on her holstered .38 revolver. Ki shook his head.

"I think no one is here, but if you wish, I'll look."

Something deep in Jessica's heart was actually relieved that Ki had offered. The wind continued to push its way through the trees and haunt the caverns above them with eerie sounds. There was no guessing what the caves might contain, and Jessie, for all the heart she had, didn't wish to find out.

It was Ki then who explored the caves, leaving Travis and Jessie below to poke around the clearing and surrounding area.

The caves were dark, but Ki could make out the crude pallets on the floor, the few bits of clothing, the dead fires. There was little else, and no one occupied the caves.

Ki, deeply puzzled, finally returned to the clearing to stand staring at the flowing river. He shook his head when Jessica asked him what he'd found.

"Nothing, nothing at all. Someone has been here of course, but they are all gone now."

"Do we wait?" Jessica asked.

"Who knows if anyone will ever return?" Kiai answered. Then he glanced at the cold gray skies. "And it will rain again, Jessica. What shall we do, take shelter in the caves? No, there's no point in waiting."

"Where in hell could they have gone?" Travis asked in a low voice. "And what can they be up to now?"

There was no way of answering the question. Ki squatted against the earth and sketched meaningless figures in the dirt as he considered their course of action.

"Perhaps," he said to Jessica, "something could be gained

by you returning to Collins to talk to the timbermen. Appeal to them somehow, tell them the witches are gone. Insult their manhood if you must, ask them what sort of children they are to let these women drive them from their work."

"A dangerous course," Travis thought.

"Yes," Jessica said thoughtfully, "but Ki may be right. We can't accomplish much up here."

"Whatever it takes to get *something* accomplished," Travis said. "We're gaining no ground whatever here—getting nothing done for the railroad or for the army."

"All right, Ki," Jessica Starbuck said. "It's back to Fort Collins then."

"For you, yes," Kiai answered and Jessica's eyes narrowed as she looked at the *te* master.

"For us?"

"Yes, I choose to remain up here. These people have gone somewhere and I mean to find them."

"We can do it together," she answered.

"No. There is no need to waste all of our resources on what may be a fruitless search. Go ahead with what we have decided, Jessie, I beg you. I have no idea if I can find them, no idea what they may be doing. Perhaps," he said, "they have gone from the mountains entirely. Who knows? But if there is a chance of it, I will try tracking them down."

"I don't like it, Ki," Jessica said, the concern in her voice obvious. "Who knows what you may run into out here?"

"Who knows indeed. Who knows what problems you might run into with the lumberjacks?" Ki smiled briefly. "All we can do is try to solve the situation, Jessica. When have we ever run away from trouble?"

Reluctantly, Jessica answered, "All right. It's logical enough, I suppose, but I don't much like the idea of having you out here on your own."

"I have," Ki replied, "been on my own for most of my life."

That was true enough, Jessica had to admit; and it had been a hard life. If there was a single man strong enough, skilled enough to defend himself against whatever might occur, it was Kiai.

She and Travis swung back into their saddles and started back toward Collins, leaving Ki alone in the desolate camp. As Jessica looked back she saw him reach down, pick up a clod of earth and crumble it in his strong hand. He knew— he knew better than she—what he was attempting and how dangerous it might be.

"There's nothing to worry about," Roger Travis told her, sensing her mood. "Nothing at all."

"No," she answered, but her smile was patently false and her words didn't ring true even to her own ears. "I know Ki. Nothing can harm him."

Ki, standing alone in the clearing, was not so sure himself. The skies, graying still more, seemed to darken his resolve as the chill wind seemed to touch his bones. Nevertheless he did what he had to do, what a man must do—he picked up the gauntlet and went on.

It wasn't difficult to pick up the sign of the women; the tracks were clear in the riverside mud. It surprised Ki to discover that there were more than twenty of them. To find so many presumably deluded young women in one group was astonishing to him.

There were several sets of larger tracks with those of the women, indicating at least two or three men had traveled with them from the cave camp.

Ki, riding slowly as the storm built again to the north, rode across the creek and into the deep woods, where the sunlight was nearly cut off by the thick upper foliage of the blue spruce and cedar.

There was no settlement that he knew of ahead, but the trail he rode now widened and lined out toward the rocky ridge ahead of him. Deeply imprinted in the trail were the footprints of many women.

And ahead the smoke rose.

Ki dipped down into the dell where the red fern flourished and followed the trail through the mountain sage and lilac toward the pine-studded knoll ahead. From there he could see the source of the smoke.

Across a deep red-stone canyon, a grassy, brushless mesa stood stark against the cobalt blue skies. There a great bonfire burned, and around the fire, as Ki squinted into the sun to watch, moved the witches.

Some of them wore black, others were naked as they moved in some weird celebration directed apparently by a tall figure standing above them on a ragged rocky outcropping. Ki slipped from the horse's back silently and moved forward on foot, his eyes narrowed, his footfalls silent.

The canyon was perhaps a quarter of a mile wide but only fifty or so feet deep, and he could see the trail that led up to the mesa across the brushy canyon, where only a trickle of cold water ran, snaking through the sage and willows.

A woman screamed and Ki started down into the canyon.

The scream was of terror and perhaps pain. It struck the ear like cold steel, and as some weird chant went up again from the fire, the scream sounded again.

Ki slid and scooted down the red-earth bank, his body sending pebbles and red dust flying. He hit the streambed solidly and wove his way through the brush, leaping the narrow stream. He found his way to the foot of the opposite trail and had started up it when the fleeing woman—rolling, stumbling, tripping—came around a bend in it toward him, the mob of witches behind her.

The girl's eyes were wide with stark fear, her dark hair

swirling, wildly wind-tangled. Her black dress sailed out behind her.

Seeing Ki she hesitated and began to halt, but the pursuit of those behind her held more fear than the tall man in front of her.

At the head of the witches was a man wearing dark trousers and a white shirt. He carried a spear made of wood, and as Ki watched he hurled it toward the girl.

"Down," Ki shouted. His hand was filled now with a deadly throwing star, and he let it fly toward the tall man. The spear landed bare inches from the girl, who had flung herself to the earth nearly at Ki's feet. The *shuriken* did not miss.

Howling with pain the tall man fell back, slapping at the shoulder where Ki's throwing star had ripped flesh and veins. At his shout the witches came to a bunched halt and began to back up the trail.

Ki reached down and yanked the black-haired girl to her feet and tugged her back down the trail. She fought him all the way, her hysterical eyes begging for help, fearing it.

The witches had gone and Ki frowned. The riverbed might have been deserted since creation as they reached it again, so silent was the day suddenly.

And then the first rocks began to rain down.

Ki was struck hard in the back by a stone and one missed his face by inches. Looking up, he saw the witches in a dark line hurling stones down at the interloper. Now a weird throaty howling had begun, and as the shower of rocks continued, the sound increased.

Ducking reflexively, Ki yanked the girl around by her arm and started off across the creekbed. A well-aimed rock from the bluff struck Ki's calf, and he winced with pain. Then the girl collapsed as a stone from the bluff smashed into her skull.

Ki swept her up, shouldering her as he made his escape through the hail of stones, splashing back across the creek.

Now the rifle fire began. Two guns at least, Ki thought, and he abandoned any thought of trying the opposite trail, where he would be an easy target. Diving into the brush, he began running upstream, weaving his way toward safety as the bullets clipped brush around him and the howling faded.

He ran on for fifteen minutes, expecting pursuit all the time. The bluff to his left began to fall away a little, and finally he saw a notch where he could leave the creek bottom. Clambering up a low, muddy bank, he entered deeper brush and then the woods beyond.

Still he saw and heard no signs of pursuit, but he couldn't congratulate himself that he'd reached safety. His horse was far downstream on the bluff, and between him and the horse were the witches and someone with rifles.

Walking a zigzag course deeper into timber, Ki breathed hard now. His heart had begun to race and his legs to grow weary. Finally he was forced to put the girl down beneath a huge pine and let her rest on the bed of pine needles there as he caught his breath and looked down his backtrail.

At first he saw nothing but the long stretch of timberland, the rise and fall of the mountains toward the purple peaks beyond. There was no sound at all but the low humming of insects, the occasional cry of a jay or the chattering of squirrels.

And then the first horse came into view and Ki smothered a curse.

The horse was a blue roan, dark mane and tail, its head held high as it walked through the pine forest. The man on its back was dressed in black and he held a rifle in his hand. Sunlight caught the rifle barrel and gleamed dully, menacingly.

Ki glanced at the dark-haired girl who lay behind him and

then looked again down the slope. The man, whoever he was, was a tracker. He was following Ki's footprints, deeply impressed in the earth because of the weight he had been carrying.

There was no way Ki was going to again shoulder the woman and be able to move with enough speed and stealth to escape the lone rider, and he knew it.

He was going to have to stand and fight and hope that *te* could somehow overcome the advantage the Winchester gave the tracker.

There was always a chance, of course; the man could be taken by surprise. Luck just might lend Kiai a hand . . . and then the second gunman appeared and Ki figured his luck had just run out.

Chapter 6

Kiai moved through the woods as silent as a shadow or a stalking panther. They had left him no choice but to fight. The woman could not be left behind and so he could not run. They had him outnumbered and outgunned. In time they would track him, and in time they would kill him if they could. That left Ki but a single option.

He would attack the stalking men.

The first of them was nearly a hundred yards up the slope from the one with the red shirt who rode more cautiously, guiding his palomino through the timber, his wary eyes shifting from point to point uncertainly.

There was a chance, Ki thought, if he could take the leader out swiftly. But his attack would need to be silent—and quite deadly.

Ki's opportunity came when the lead horseman dipped into a dell while the following rider was momentarily lost in timber. The first man, following Ki's tracks exactly, not trying to outguess his quarry or shortcut the trail, would pass beneath the great pine where Ki now pointed himself.

With his eyes constantly shuttling to the slope below him and back, Kiai climbed the tree nearly as swiftly as the silver squirrel that scampered up ahead of him, scolding, tail curled over its back.

Easing out onto the middle of the heavy bough, Ki waited

silently, his blood pulsing in his temples, his muscles tight with tension.

The lead rider rose up out of the dell, his spurred heels touching the flanks of his roan, his eyes still down, following the tracks of the man he hunted. The rifle, held in his right hand, was cocked, ready for a snap shot at the first sign of trouble. The eyes of the hunter could not be made out beneath the brim of his wide hat. Shadow covered half of his face, but the jawline, Ki saw, was firm, the wide mouth set. He seemed to be half-Indian at least. He rode well, tracked skillfully and was resolute on his job—to kill the stranger.

Each step the walking horse took now seemed slower as the roan and its deadly rider moved nearer to the great pine. Ki stilled his breath and prepared his body, knowing the risk he was taking. If the man was as competent as he appeared it would be no easy task to take him unaware. Down the slope now the second tracker dipped into the little dell, briefly disappearing from Ki's view.

The first tracker was no more than twenty feet away from the perch where Ki had been waiting, when the woman on the ground behind the martial-arts master cried out, groaning loudly then shrilling a pained sound.

The hunter's head came up and he smiled crookedly, kneeing his horse, urging it on, the rifle coming up at the ready as he dropped the reins, letting the pony have its head.

A foot more—the horse seemed to move that slowly as Ki waited, praying the tracker wouldn't glance up—and then another, and the horse and rider were both beneath the pine bough where Kiai waited.

He hurled himself from the bough, and as the rider's head came up and around, his mouth twisting into a sneer, the Winchester beginning to lift, Ki's heel slammed into his jaw, smashing his head to one side, driving the tracker from the saddle as the horse reared, whinnying loudly, shrilly.

47

Ki rolled aside as the horse flailed out with its forehoofs and the stunned tracker dove for the rifle he had lost. Ki was to his feet first, and as the Indian tracker tried to snatch up his Winchester, Ki side-kicked him, his slippered foot driving against the hunter's heart with sledgehammer force.

The tracker's finger managed to touch the trigger of the rifle, and a .44–40 slug whined off through the forest, striking living wood, causing bark to explode from the base of a big pine. The second tracker then lifted his horse into an uphill run, bringing his own rifle from its sheath to shoulder and aim at Ki.

Ki grabbed the fallen rifle from the ground and, holding it by the barrel, sent it whirling through the air. It was as deadly and as stunning as a bullet when it caught the second rider in the throat and sent him cartwheeling backward from his horse, his neck shattered by the impact of walnut and steel.

Neither man on the ground moved. The palomino had bolted, but the roan, after some momentary excitement, had settled and now stood, head down, picking at some tufts of grass on the open patches between the pines.

Ki moved toward it, speaking softly, and took up the reins, leading it back to where the woman on the ground had begun to stir, to lift herself to a sitting position and lean against the tree, holding her head.

"Who are you?" she asked, her eyes moving uncomfortably from Ki to the distance.

"Just a stranger. Your head hurts. Let me see it."

"What happened?" she asked, recoiling a little as Ki's fingers gently moved across her skull, finding the egg-sized, bleeding lump there.

"They were throwing rocks, don't you remember?" Ki replied. He sat back on his heels. "It's not fractured, I don't think. You were lucky."

48

"Lucky!" The woman spat out a laugh, which seemed to cause her head to ache even more. She briefly buried her face in her hands. Her dark hair, tangled with pine needles now, covered one eye as she lifted her face again. "How could you call this luck?" She looked back toward the river bottom. "Will they be coming after me?"

"I don't know. We have one horse. We ought to try to get out of the area, find a safe place to rest for you while I double back and see if there are more people following us."

"All right . . ." Again her head sagged. "I'm sorry," she apologized. "I know you want me to get up, to be moving. If you could just help me to my feet . . ."

Ki stood and lifted her gently. For just a moment she leaned against him and recovered herself. Her body was lithe, full-breasted and slim-hipped. Her hair, despite its disarray held a clean scent. She seemed ready to cling to him for just a second and then shook her head as if to clear it and stepped back, smiling faintly.

"All right. I'll go with you. Whatever you say. Just take me away from here—from them."

"Are you not one of *them*?" Ki asked.

"I don't know, I don't know!" She ran her fingers through her hair in puzzlement. "I was there—that is all. I was there."

"All right. We have to travel now." Ki paused. "You haven't told me your name."

"My real name is Rebecca. Rebecca, though that's not what they called me up there."

Ki asked for no explanation of that. He imagined that all things "up there" were different than they were in the real world. He swung up onto the roan's back and helped Rebecca up behind him, and then with the cold wind still blowing, with the two dead men on the ground behind them, they started off into the higher reaches of the mountains.

And somewhere yet behind them the witches still roamed as the dark clouds began to gather once more and a new storm to build in the north.

Jessica Starbuck shook her head, looked skyward and turned to Roger Travis. "It's a waste of our time to continue, a total waste of time."

Travis nodded in solemn agreement. Bob Sachs shrugged as if to say "I told you so."

The meeting held on the edge of town for the striking timbermen had done nothing at all to resolve their complaints. Nothing would bring them back on the job, not gold or threats or promises, until they had been assured that the witches had deserted the mountains once and for all.

Jessica had gone far, knowing how important the workers were to the future of the railroad, promising them all large bonuses, but they were unshakable in their refusal to return to the job. Later she had begged them to consider the welfare of their families, but that did no good either, and in the end, frustrated, she had turned her back to them, waved her hands in the air and left it to Roger Travis to berate them.

"What's the matter with you men—if you call yourselves men these days? Hiding out in town, letting a bunch of women run you out of the hills, out of your jobs, out of your self-respect!"

"You go up there, Mister, if you think it's something you want to face!"

The answering voice came from one of the Welsh miners. As Jessica and Travis talked to them, they had bunched up to one side of the loading dock they were using as a platform. On the other side, the mostly Chinese crowd watched and listened.

"Listen . . . ." Travis began, but the lumberman cut him off sharply.

"You listen, my friend. You can call them a bunch of women and let it go at that, but we know what they are." That brought a murmur of assent from the men around the man who spoke. "They are evil and the things they do in the night are evil. I tell you the truth. Satan is their leader and Satan sends them out in the night to kill and do mayhem. You try cutting timber with one hand on your gun and the other on your rosary to fend off them witches. You just try it," he finished soberly.

Travis turned toward Jessica and made a palms-up gesture signifying that he too had given up. The jacks and mill workers couldn't be bribed or bullied or humiliated into returning to work.

All that remained was to drive the coven from the hills, and with the total lack of help from the authorities it seemed an unlikely task. True, Jessica could have brought in some more of her own people from Kansas, but by the time they arrived it might already be too late, the winter might have set in, closing all hopes of extending the line to Vasquez that year and effectively destroying the profitability of the Comstock Central as the army looked elsewhere for its beef supply.

They tried the sheriff again.

The man looked comfortable in his warm office, sitting with his boots propped up on a dully glowing iron stove, puffing on his pipe as the cold winds blew outside.

He only blinked as Jessie and Travis entered, allowing a gust of wind into the office. He looked Jessica up and down and finally made a vague gesture with his pipe, and the two visitors took seats in the wooden chairs indicated.

"I 'spect I know what this is about, Miss Starbuck."

"Yes, I expect you do," Jessica answered. There was an edge to her voice, and the sheriff frowned, taking his pipe briefly from his mouth to study the bowl as if he had never seen such a thing before. He replaced it in his teeth before he answered, talking around the stem.

"There's nothing I can do," the lawman answered, rumpling his already disordered thin red hair. "Told your friend here, I've got my town to take care of, and the mountains." He shrugged. "They've got to get by on their own up there.

"Besides, if all those growed men can't defend themselves against a handful of women, I'm damned if I'd stir to help them anyway."

"There have been crimes committed up there," Travis said. The young army officer was near the boiling point. If he had been more frustrated in his career he couldn't remember when. Sent to accomplish a simple mission, he was falling on his face in Fort Collins.

"Don't doubt it," the sheriff said dryly. "But then there's a use for rough justice, and maybe somebody ought to look to it. I'll say it again—what goes on in them mountains is not my affair, and I'm not going up there and leaving this town."

"Or your stove," Travis said under his breath and Jessica shot him a quelling glance. It wasn't going to do them any good to alienate the sheriff.

She leaned forward and tried one of her very best smiles. "There must be men around town who would be willing to form a posse if the rewards were big enough."

"No, there ain't," the lawman answered. He removed his pipe, spat out a piece of burned tobacco, rubbed his tongue and shook his head.

"With a reward," Jessica insisted, "there's usually men enough to go into anything."

"Let me ask you this, Miss," the sheriff said, dropping his feet to the floor, "just who are you raising a posse against? Far as I can see if you set out with some kind of hunting party, some lynch mob, you'll be breaking the law in my town, raising such a party.''

Travis tried to interrupt angrily, but the sheriff lifted a silencing hand. ''You got a warrant, for example? You got a witness to a certain crime, someone who will name me a name? I'm sorry, Miss, genuinely sorry. I don't need all these extra men hanging around my town—in the end that will make more trouble—but you ain't raising no posse without some cause you can show me.

''You could find men, I guess, and find them without me knowing about it—maybe. But you wouldn't find good, hard-working, honest men who got their jobs and family to tend to; you'd find a bunch of gun-carrying drifters who's as soon shoot *you* as a witch. Any man who'd agree to go out hunting down women ain't a man you want for the job anyway.''

Again Travis tried to interrupt; again it was useless. ''Also,'' the lawman went on, ''consider this, Miss. If you don't kill these women off—for which I'd arrest you, and properly—just what are you going to do with them? Round them up and bring them into me to lock up? Where? And with my male prisoners? And on what charges? You can't charge a group of people with a single crime, and you ain't give me a name or individual charge yet.''

The sheriff had obviously given the problem more thought than Jessica Starbuck would have guessed, perhaps more than she had. He continued, ''And if you try to round them up, throw them on that train of yours, transporting them out of the mountains, Miss, why then who's breaking the law? And we do still have laws against kidnapping in Colorado.

''No, Miss,'' he concluded, ''I can't help you, and frankly, I don't see what you can do to help yourself out of this.''

Travis was gloomy. They stood outside the sheriff's office as light, cold rain began to fall and sunset expanded its deep orange colors across the sky.

"I could almost strangle the sheriff," Travis said. "The trouble is, he's right in a lot of ways. What, for instance, could the army do down here? Send a picket line through their camp and shoot them down? Apply martial law? Damn it all, Jessica, we've got a problem there doesn't seem to be a solution to. Personally, I'm stuck for an answer."

"Let's get something to eat," Jessica suggested. "Have dinner and a lot of coffee, a good night's sleep. Maybe something will occur to us." She was obviously as stumped as Travis, but she was unwilling to admit there was no solution to any problem. That wasn't the way Alex Starbuck had raised her. You fought and you fought hard and if you got knocked down you picked yourself up and had another try.

Dinner sounded good and the coffee better as the rain increased and the brief mountain sunset faded behind the massing gray clouds. Jessica was deeply thoughtful and Roger Travis thought he knew what was troubling her.

"Ki?" he asked.

"Yes. It's going to rain again and he's out there." She lifted her head and offered a quick smile to the young army officer. "But he'll be all right. Ki is always all right."

She didn't know about the stalkers.

Chapter 7

Ki again lifted his eyes to the silent, wind-bent forest. With the loss of daylight it was becoming more and more difficult to make them out as they stalked the *te* master and his witch companion. Ki withdrew toward the small lean-to he had built for the girl earlier when the rain first began to fall and it was obvious she could go no farther.

Earlier they had talked and Ki had learned a great deal, enough to make him even more wary than he had been.

"You said you did not know if you were one of them or not," Ki had remarked as the woman, sitting on the pine needle–covered earth had watched his expert hands weave pine branches together over a rude lodgepole forming the lean-to where he intended the girl to sleep. "How can this be? And what is it you did to make them turn on you?"

"I tried to leave," the girl said with a yawn. "That is forbidden, of course, for if one leaves, two might leave, or many, and then the coven is broken. 'Rebecca,' the warlock told me, 'you may try to leave, but you will be painfully sorry if you try it. Our Dark Master will not allow it. Nor will I.'"

"But," Ki said to Rebecca, "you tried to leave anyway."

"Yes." She lifted those dark, pained eyes to Ki. "You cannot imagine how terrible it has become. There is torture and murder—unspeakable things. Once they found a three-year-old Indian child wandering . . ." her voice broke off. "I had to try to leave no matter the consequences."

"How did this warlock of yours ever convince you all to come here to this desolate country—and with winter approaching?" Ki asked, stepping away from his work briefly to study it at a distance. He wore a puzzled look as he asked the question. There was little he had not seen in his wandering life, but this he did not understand.

"There are men like that, Ki," Rebecca told him. "You are a man and not a woman, and so you do not understand perhaps. There are men who can tell women to leap from cliffs and they will do it. Men who can batter a woman, torture her and be loved and admired for it. Manning is one of those."

"That is the warlock's name?"

"Yes." Her head bobbed almost imperceptibly. "That is his name. He may tell a woman to kill and she will kill. He may tell her to follow him into the desolate mountains and she will. Perhaps it is that all of the women are sick; perhaps he has some secret power—the power that he tells them comes from the Dark Master."

"Satan, you mean."

Again the slight bob of the head. "Yes," the dark-haired young woman said, "just so. Satan."

Ki had returned to his work and now he spoke with his back to her. In the saddlebags of the tracker's horse they had found bacon, biscuits, beans and a blanket. Now, sitting on the blanket as a light mist began to fall, Rebecca munched on one of the salt biscuits as they talked.

"Where do these women come from?" Ki asked.

"Everywhere. Some from the streets, some from fine homes and families."

"And you?" Ki asked.

56

"A good home so far as money went. My mother was a dear woman but weak. My father was too strong, too cruel."

"And so he has brought you all here. How do you live?"

"We steal for Manning. We rob people," the girl said with a disgusted shrug. "Those who do very well are rewarded by the warlock with his special favors."

"What favors are those?"

"What do you think? They are allowed to share his bed and receive Satan's seed."

A dirty portrait of a half-sane megalomaniac was beginning to form itself in Ki's mind. The man was a womanizer, a butcher, a criminal. And, Ki suspected, the reason he had no fear of being caught for any crime was that none of his deluded followers would ever give evidence against him, out of a sort of dark love—and stark fear.

"I still do not understand why this Manning brought his coven here, to these high mountains," Ki said, finishing his work to sit cross-legged beside the girl. "I do not understand why he terrorizes the timber camp, why I was attacked."

"You don't, really?" Rebecca responded. "It's simple, Ki. Didn't you notice the men who tried to attack you? Western men. They are men used to guns, more dangerous than a few women with rocks. Cattlemen, Ki. They are hired guns for a cattleman. Even now a herd is being held in a near valley. When the railroad is unable to complete its contract, the cattle will be driven to Fort Vasquez. The cost will be outrageous, but the army will have little choice but to buy the beef."

Ki's eyes opened a little wider. Now he had something he could grasp. Before it had been difficult for him to understand any of this, to find the handle for the seemingly meaningless terrorizing of the timber camp, the presence of the witches' coven. Explained, it became simple, if devious and unique.

Once the cause behind the bizarre effect was understood, it all became obvious.

"Manning will receive a cut from the cattle sale, of course," Ki said, thinking aloud. "The cattleman—what is his name?"

"Carl Dantley," the woman replied.

"I haven't heard the name. Perhaps Jessica will know it."

"Jessica," the girl said, lowering her eyes, "the blond woman, you mean?"

"Yes, Jessica Starbuck."

"Are you and she . . . ?"

"Lovers?" Ki answered. "No. I am her friend, her employee if you like. Once long ago I was hired by her father to act as her protector—but my story is too long. Yours is the one that must be told."

"There is no more," Rebecca said. "Dantley and Manning met somehow and the plan was proposed. Dantley lost the contract to Starbuck and was in a fury. Apparently he had once delivered infected beef to the army, and they would have nothing to do with him, even with talking to him. He decided to get even and make a huge profit at once. Manning is always more than willing to turn a dollar no matter what it takes. The cattleman hired some gunmen and bribed them with the promise of free women, which Manning supplies, and with the promise of easy money. We were brought here to frighten away the superstitious and to do whatever it took to get rid of those who could not be frightened away . . . and," the girl said with a sigh of anger at herself, "we did it."

"There will be more men after us then," Ki said. "You know too much, and they will want to silence both of us. For now, though," Ki said, looking to the darkening skies and the rain, which was increasing, "you must try to rest. I will stand watch."

Rebecca nodded dreamily. She was exhausted, obviously, and even the dread she carried with her could not keep her awake for much longer.

"There is the blanket," Ki said. "Take the food if you wish to eat more before you sleep. I will wake you if there is trouble. Rebecca? Have you another name?" he asked.

"Yes, of course," she answered. "Manning. My name is Rebecca Manning. So you see, Ki, I had no choice in this, did I? Where my father went, so must I go."

Then lightly she touched his arm and went into the lean-to, leaving Ki to his vigil and his thoughts.

Two hours later they came.

Ki could hear precious little above the wind and the rain. Oddly it was the smell of damp horses that alerted him first. He knew he and Rebecca would be difficult if not impossible to find on a night like this—with the clouds screening out the stars and rain veiling the world so that even the tree next to Ki was nearly invisible—but you never knew. Their pursuers could stumble into the camp, perhaps decide to swing from leather themselves and camp within yards of where Ki had built his lean-to.

They would have to be taken out.

For the same reason, although Ki still had the Winchester he had captured from the first tracker, he chose to move without a firearm. Striking in silence from the night gave him an advantage, he thought. The muzzle flash from his rifle would draw return fire instantly. What they did not see, they could not target.

Ki was determined they would not see him.

He could not tell how many of them were out there. Perhaps a few, perhaps many. He began to move toward the sound of the horse he now heard, his trained body catlike and silent. Rain misted through the trees, covering his movements further, soaking his clothing through.

He came suddenly upon the horseman. Out of the darkness and rain the rider appeared no more than fifteen feet from Ki. The hunter pawed at his side arm, sheltered beneath the yellow slicker he wore, but he never touched the butt of his gun. A *shuriken* sang softly through the air, and the deadly blades ripped open his throat.

The rider fell softly to the ground, his horse sidestepping away in confusion.

To Ki's left was another horse, and he stepped behind a huge spruce to conceal himself. This hunter carried his rifle in its scabbard to protect it from the rain, across the withers of his horse. He never saw Ki.

The *te* master slipped from behind the tree as the stalker passed him. Kiai took four long running steps and leaped for the rider's throat. His arm hooked around the man's neck in passing, and they fell to the ground. The stalker tried to come up with a knife, but Ki's forearm smashed into his nose, driving bone up into the cowboy's brain, and the man lay still and quiet, dead against the damp mountain earth.

Breathing hard, Ki stood and listened, his eyes searching the forest. He heard nothing, sensed no other presence. Two more he had killed. And in the morning would there be two more and again two more? There would have to be.

The rancher, Dantley, and Manning, the warlock, could not allow Ki to escape. And with the coming of day, the odds would all be in their favor. Grimly Ki returned to the lean-to, where the exhausted woman had managed to fall asleep, and with his head and shoulders just inside the shelter he had built, he sat to wait out the long, deadly night.

Jessica Starbuck smiled. Roger Travis was snoring quietly, his body and mind at total ease after a long night of love-making. The night was still; only the sound of rain could be heard.

What then had awakened her?

A sudden feeling of discomfort came over her. *Something* was not quite right. Feeling slightly foolish, she slipped nude from the bed and went to her holster, which hung on the wooden chair across the room. In it was the .38 revolver her father had had made especially for her by Samuel Colt's New York company. Slate gray, the gun was mounted on a .44 frame to reduce the kick. Jessie was more than familiar with the weapon. It had been a friend, an ally, a comfort to her many times in many places.

Still feeling slightly foolish, she returned to the bed, placed the gun under the pillow and rolled toward the sleeping army officer.

He had satisfied her body earlier, but she could feel unmistakable returning desire, and as her hand trailed up his long hard thigh to his groin and touched him intimately, he began to respond, although he was still asleep. Jessie wrapped her hand around his swelling manhood and gently tugged at him, her nibbling lips nuzzling his neck and ears until Travis turned toward her and nearly devoured her mouth with an urgent kiss.

His erection was solid now, and Jessica toyed with him as she rolled onto her back and looked up into his suddenly alert eyes. Her palm cupped his sack as she kissed him intently and his hand found her breast and tightly gripped it, his thumb running over her aroused nipple.

Her head lifted to kiss his chest and then fell back onto the pillow as Travis lifted his body and centered it between her thighs, which spread, lifted and admitted him into her softening, moist body.

It was then that the door crashed open and the witches swarmed into the room.

They carried clubs and rocks, and as Travis lifted himself and tried to spin toward them, one of the stones cracked against his skull and sent him slumping to the floor still tangled in the bedsheets.

Jessica shouted wildly and reached for the .38 Colt, bringing it up to fire three rapid shots, at least one tagging flesh as a witch screamed with pain and thudded back against the wall.

But she could do no more. There were six or seven women on Jessica by then, a chattering, murmuring, chanting swarm of them, beating her with their hands, ripping the gun from her grip, wrapping her in the blankets of the bed before they lifted her and carried her from the room and out into the dark Colorado night.

Chapter 8

Dawn broke red and blurred as the rain clouds hovered over the deep forest where Ki had built his lean-to. The squirrels, eager to feed after the rain, raced through the trees around him and picked at the pinecones, extracting the nuts. To the west a flight of geese, heading south, cut a V against the gray skies.

The mountains stood in stony allegiance beyond the lower hills, immortal masters of their lonely world.

The girl shook, lifted one eyelid, quivered again and then sat up to look at Ki as one stunned from a blow. "You . . ." was all she said.

"Yes, it is I. It was no dream, unfortunately," Ki answered.

She was pensive, rising slowly as she came out of the lean-to to look at the murky morning skies. Her hands rose and fell, slapping against her thighs in a gesture of frustration. She whirled to face Ki.

"It's hopeless, isn't it? We can't escape. All that's happened is that I've dragged you into this mess."

"I was involved in it before our paths crossed," Ki answered. "It is not your fault."

"They'll never let me escape," Rebecca said, turning her back, crossing her arms beneath her breasts. "But you—you could make it by yourself. I could lead them off!" she said with sudden wild inspiration.

"Don't think of such things," Ki answered quietly. "I will not leave you here alone."

The girl faced him again and moved a step toward him, asking, "What kind of man are you?" as her eyes searched those of Ki.

"I hope a good man. One who will not surrender to those who would harm a woman or murder a man."

"Then one day you'll die because of the kind of man you are," Rebecca finally responded.

"One day I shall die," Ki agreed. "But I will not go out as a coward or as one who did not do his duty."

"You have no duty toward me!" the witch said with a short, bitter laugh.

"There is always duty," Ki replied. "Always duty and always honor if one is a man."

"I've never met anyone like you," Rebecca said with a wondering shake of her head.

"Then I am sorry for you. I am not a special man in many ways. The West is filled with men of honor and of strength. It is just that I am here, that I have chosen to shelter you and do what is right. I will not leave you. It is beneath a man to do such a thing."

They had two horses now and still more provisions. They carried two Winchester repeating .44–40 rifles. None of this lent Kiai any sense of confidence. Between themselves and Fort Collins an unknown number of hunters rode the hills.

To ride to the north and circle toward town would force them to travel through the land claimed by Nataka, who was of uncertain disposition. To ride southward pushed them through the very land Carl Dantley had chosen to hold his herd on. To the east was the coven of witches, to the west the vast high reaches of the Rocky Mountains.

There was no good alternative. Only a succession of bad chances.

"Which way then?" Rebecca asked after a time. She could sense that Ki was pondering their choices, finding none of them to his liking.

"South," he said at length, and after a long slow breath. "We ride south, Rebecca."

She didn't question his decision. He was the man she had allowed to take command of her destiny, and his decision was law.

The skies were clearing again as they rode the long mountain meadows. Still stacked clouds rode through the blue above the mountains, but they carried no rain now. They seemed more like wandering sheep looking for a resting place.

Now and then they began to see stray cattle, and as they rode the fringe of the forest and sat their horses overlooking a vast green valley, they saw the main herd. There were five hundred or so of them grazing lazily as cowboys rode their rounds in slow circles, keeping them bunched. Once Ki heard the squalling sound of a calf being branded, but aside from that the valley was silent.

"Does Dantley have a house here?" Ki asked.

"I think so. A little farther on by the creek, although I've never been there. My father said something about sitting down to dinner with him. Why?"

"It would be interesting to have a talk with him," Ki said, but Rebecca couldn't penetrate what was going on in his mind.

"It would be a waste of time," she protested. "What could you charge him with that he couldn't deny? He has every right to hold his cattle wherever he likes."

That was the frustrating part of it all, Ki thought. There was no direct crime the cattleman could be charged with; no way to implicate Manning directly in any of the witches' crimes.

They continued on, sticking to the forest verge. Ki casually, almost subconsciously, counted the number of men Carl Dantley had working for him and noted that they were far more than were needed to work the cattle. They were a small army. Both men, Dantley and Manning, were intent on their plan to close down the railroad and reap the benefits in the form of a huge cattle sale. They were risking a lot; they wouldn't give it up easily.

A lone cowhand, looking for strays apparently, rode toward them, his pinto pony moving slowly up a grassy dell, and Ki kept Rebecca's horse back along with his. The man, a youth really, with blond hair showing on his forehead beneath his hat, rode past them, whistling, never seeing them or suspecting there might be an enemy in the woods.

Now, ahead and to the east, Ki could see the crude log houses where the cattlemen had taken up temporary residence. He looked to the mountains, picking out a few landmarks for the day he would return there. Now his only thought was getting Rebecca Manning to safety.

He wanted to reach Collins by this circuitous route, coordinate with Jessica and together formulate a plan of attack. By now, he believed, knowing Jessica, she had found some way to get the timbermen back to work and was probably impatiently awaiting Ki's return.

He and Rebecca would not be able to ride through the night in unfamiliar country with weary horses, and that meant yet another night in dangerous territory. There was no telling how many trackers were following them, if any. Each time they crested out a ridge or topped a hill, Ki was careful to pause and look down their backtrail. He saw no one, but he was well aware that it meant nothing. The timber could hide much.

They rode through the day in virtual silence. Kiai didn't press the girl to speak of what she had been through or to probe her thoughts. He was intent now only on survival.

It was nearly dark when they crossed the river again. Enough dusky light still colored the skies so that Ki could make out the caves, similar to those at the witches' camp, that seemed to proliferate along the broad river's bluffs.

"We'll have to shelter up there," Ki said.

"All right," Rebecca answered, and there was a touch of nervousness in her voice.

"Does it bring back bad memories?"

"It's all right," she said, but she sat her saddle rigidly and stared straight ahead. Ki wondered what she had seen and heard in those other, upstream caves.

They were lucky that, in an area just off the gravel beach of the river, they found a cave big enough to shelter the horses. The mouth of the cave was screened off with willow brush, providing some security. Branching off from the large cavern was a smaller cave where Ki took the saddlebags, which still contained food, their canteens and the bedrolls captured from the stalkers he had killed.

There he made a bed for each of them and started a small, smoky fire with driftwood and twigs pack rats had dragged into the cave. The smoke rose lazily and escaped somewhere above. Ki was not the first to have used the cave for shelter. Indians at one time, perhaps in the far distant past, had used the caves for dwellings, for there was much smoke on the walls, and here and there a pictograph scratched into the cavern clay.

The woman lay down without eating, the dull glow of the tiny fire glossing her face with color, tinting and streaking her hair with highlights. Ki sat near the fire, feeding it carefully, thinking his own thoughts. On this night he wondered if Jessica, in her Collins hotel room, thought about whether he were alive or dead, and he wondered what progress she had made in solving the labor problem at Game Trail Camp. He wondered, too, if Travis had managed to get help from the army and if the sheriff had decided finally to cooperate in cleaning out the mess in the mountains.

And he wondered if the hunters were still behind him, still on his trail, coming with their thunder guns and witches' clubs.

"Ki?"

The voice was so soft that at first Ki was not sure if he had heard her at all, or only a word murmured in her sleep, but as he glanced toward her bed he saw her fire-bright eyes on him.

"What is it?"

"The night is a frightening one, and I'm cold." She hesitated before she went on. "Will you lie down beside me and give me comfort?"

"Are you sure?" he asked and the woman answered positively.

"Yes, I am sure."

Sitting up, she pulled her dark dress off over her head. She wore nothing beneath it. Her breasts were very white, flawless, of medium size, uptilted, capped by pink nipples which now stood taut. She cupped her hands to her own breasts and asked Ki, "Can you not use some comfort, too?"

"Yes," he answered softly, "I, too, can use some comfort on this night."

Then he stood before the fire, slipped off his vest and unbuttoned his red shirt. The woman's eyes brightened still more, and not from the firelight as Ki kicked off his slippers, unbuckled his belt and let his jeans fall to the floor. He heard her breath catch as she caught sight of his swelling erection, and as he moved toward her, Rebecca's eyes had difficulty drawing away from its fascination.

She sat up, and as Ki stood before her, she wrapped her arms around his thighs, her hands clutching his buttocks, and her lips moved lightly across his thighs and groin, inflaming his erection still more. Then, throwing her blanket aside, she lay back and summoned Ki with one finger.

He went to her, subtly and slowly arousing her, kissing her ankles and calves, letting his hand roam the length of her thighs before he got to his knees and, hovering over her, looked down into her eyes as his two strong hands found her breasts.

Slowly, inexorably her thighs spread and, touching her once between her legs, Ki found the warm dampness of her.

"Ki," she said, her voice only a hoarse whisper, "do it to me, please."

Ki sat down facing her, his legs crossed. Gently but with firm authority he lifted her hips and slid her toward him until she was sitting on his lap facing him, her naked body pressed to his, her fire-bright face soft with emotion.

Ki lifted her body, and she reached down to find his erection and slip it home, sighing with pleasure as she settled on its length.

The fire flickered and the woman swayed, leaning back, her hands clutching Ki's shoulders. She bit at her lower lip and rocked her head back, making small, happy sounds as her body softened and sagged and became wetter still.

She could stand no more of it and flopped onto her back, taking Ki with her. Her legs were uplifted, straight at the knee and spread widely as Ki penetrated her deeply, working himself in slow circles, his mouth bruising hers with passion.

She worked against him, touching him where he entered her, fingering herself until she finished with a shuddering sigh seconds before Ki reached his own powerful climax. The woman lay back, eyes closed as Ki continued to gently rock against her, his hands roaming her smooth white shoulders and breasts.

The fire burned low and the wind outside began to howl, but neither of them noticed it. As the fire burned out, so did passion, and they fell asleep with deep contentment.

With the dawn the gunmen appeared.

Chapter 9

The first man into the cave was big, burly, and he had a large blue Colt revolver in his hand, the hammer drawn back, his eyes dangerously set. The second man was much smaller, less dangerous-appearing, but his .44 revolver was just as big. Ki made hardly a movement.

"The ladies are always a good man's downfall," the big man said to Ki. "Hard to keep alert, ain't it?" The tone of voice was part sneer, part the respect one fighting man gives to another. "You wasn't easy to track, friend, but Dan Fellows keeps on a trail once he starts. I guess your luck run out. How about slipping into your pants? Then you can hold a blanket up in front of the lady while she dresses.

"Just don't make any mistakes, friend. I was raised a gentleman by my mama, but I learned plenty of other sorts of skills along the way."

"I will make no mistake," Ki answered. The man, vast and redheaded, smiled faintly as he talked, but there was little doubt in Kiai's mind that he had used the Colt before and would again with the slightest incentive.

Ki stepped into his jeans and buttoned them up. He reached for his shirt and vest then, but Fellows told his companion: "Archie, run through his gear first. No one wants any shooting in here. Hate ricochets—never know who they'll tag."

The man called Archie, slim and nervous, moved to Ki's

71

gear and picked up the two rifles. Ki's knife was next, and then the gunman picked up and hefted Ki's leather vest. It was too heavy, and it clinked slightly as he did so. Archie made a small wondering sound.

"What the hell . . . ?" he said, and he backed away with the rifles under his arm, vest in his hand.

"What'd you find, Archie?" Dan Fellows asked.

"Don't know for sure." Archie dipped a hand into one of the many hidden pockets of the leather vest and withdrew it rapidly. Blood trickled from his finger and thumb where a *shuriken* had slashed his hand. "Son of a bitch!" the gun-fighter shouted, shaking the blood off his hand. "What are those?"

He handed the vest over to Dan Fellows, who seemed mildly amused but was still watching Ki with deadly concentration. Gingerly he extracted one of the throwing stars and hefted it in his palm. He smiled a little more deeply as he intensified his study of Ki.

"I don't know what these are; I don't know who you are, mister, but I'm sure you'll bear some watching. I'm damn sure you'll bear some watching." He paused. Then with a shrug he said, "I'm sure you've got some kind of trick up your sleeve that you're just aching to try out. I wouldn't. You might get me. Hell, might get Archie, too, but there's three men with repeating rifles outside, and it don't matter what kind of trick it is, you don't have a chance, so let's make it as peaceful as possible, all right?"

"Yes," Ki agreed. He, too, recognized a warrior when he saw one. Fellows would not be easily tricked, nor would he be backed down. He held a blanket up in front of Rebecca as she slipped into her dress. Remarkably, Archie blushed and turned his head slightly away. Dan Fellows gaze held steady, but not on Rebecca. He watched Ki, only Ki, the hands of the man, his eyes.

"Why are you doing this?" Ki asked as Rebecca, in her dress now, allowed him to drop and fold the blanket. "You must have a reason for hunting the woman down?"

"I'm working for a living, friend, that's all," Dan Fellows said. "A man's got to live. It's not personal. All I know is the boss says you two have a scheme up to drift his herd."

"What do you mean?" Ki asked, his eyes growing harder now. Fellows hadn't budged an inch in the last ten minutes. He held his gun as steadily as ever, leveled at Ki's belly. "Do you mean Dantley has told you we're out to rustle his cattle?"

"That's it in a nutshell," Fellows said. Archie, still appearing nervous, was holding his pistol beside his leg. Rebecca, after a disgusted snort at Fellows' explanation, was tugging her boots on and buttoning them.

"It's not true, you know," Ki said, but Fellows just shook his head at the disclaimer.

"I don't know. Maybe not. The law'll decide, I reckon."

"The law!" Rebecca said suddenly, shrilly. "What do you think they have in mind for us? Some sort of trial? It's my father who's behind this, and I know him well enough to tell you that he'll never let Ki near a court or a lawman! You're nothing but a hired killer!"

Fellows looked honestly baffled. "I don't know, lady. I work for the brand, that's all. The boss tells me the Chinaman here and this rich lady he works for are out to break him, to run off his herd so's they can bring their own cattle into the army post. I work for him, like I say. He pays me good and I believe him."

Rebecca made the same disgusted sound and turned away, folding her arms. Ki spoke quietly.

"I am not," he said first of all, "a Chinaman. Nor am I a cattle thief. The lady I work for is just that—a lady. She is not a thief either."

73

"I dunno," Fellows said with a shake of his head. "I just know I get paid to protect the herd, to fight for the brand. That's what I'm doing, friend. You got something to say, you say it to the boss."

Ki had to admire and pity the man at once. He appeared to be a straightforward cowboy, but a man whose loyalty was so intense that it was easy for him to be deluded by whatever Carl Dantley said. He was clearly being used; clearly there was no way to talk him out of what he believed his duty to be. There was nothing for Ki to do but button his shirt, take Rebecca's hand and under the muzzle of the gun-fighters' guns, walk from the cave into the bright, clear light of the Colorado morning. There were three men out there, waiting and watching expectantly, and as Ki and Rebecca swung into leather these filed in behind them, following with unsheathed guns as Dan Fellows led the way to the Dantley ranchhouse in the long valley.

From without, the house seemed like nothing more than rows of unbarked logs set among uprights, topped off by a suspiciously sagging sod roof. There was more to it as Ki found out when he was helped roughly from the saddle and taken into Carl Dantley's house followed by Rebecca and Dan Fellows, whose Colt was again drawn from its holster.

The walls of the house were paneled with varnished cedar. Indian blankets were scattered across the floor, and on a heavy, rough-hewn cedar table two brass bookends in the shape of archers supported three leather-bound volumes. The fireplace was massive, of native stone, topped by a cedar mantel where a few Indian artifacts sat. Above these on the chimney was an ancient Hall breechloader. It seemed that Dantley had come into the country with the intention of staying. And why not? A steady market for his beef would provide for him as long as he chose to pursue it.

It occurred to Ki that if the man had gone about business

74

legally he might have done as well. But with Starbuck beating him to the army contract, he had a huge investment standing to be lost.

Dantley himself limped down a long hallway and entered the room. He grunted, gestured limply to one of his men and had a puncheon rocking chair scooted up behind him. He sat and glared at Ki and Rebecca.

A long, gaunt man with one eye, which lacked any sign of luster, he was dark-haired, hollow-cheeked, a man whose jawline showed no evidence it had ever been tortured into a smile.

"Good work, Dan," he said to Fellows. "Got the son of a bitch, you did."

"A little luck and some good tracking by Archie," Fellows said modestly.

"There'll be a little something extra in both your pay this month," Dantley said. His dead eye shifted from Fellows to Ki, and his mouth tightened into an ugly curve. "You've done murder, my friend. I suppose you know what happens to people who do murder on my range."

"I know what you would like to do," Ki answered calmly. "But I am no murderer."

Rebecca, trembling, stood near to Ki, clutching his hand with all of her strength. The crooked, mock smile fell from Dantley's face as he answered.

"You lie, damn you! You killed Bart Glover and Frank Sanderson. You killed Tom Gear . . ."

"These men were trying to kill me," Ki said evenly. "And the woman, possibly."

"The woman! This poor demented girl that you either kidnapped or seduced away from her natural father!"

"I hardly think she is demented," Ki replied. "As for kidnapping her, that too is a lie, as you know. She was running for her life from her 'natural father.' You know full

75

well what sort of man he is, Mr. Dantley. And you know your reasons for wishing to kill me have nothing to do with either of these charges."

"No," Dantley said with cynicism, "I just kill for the hell of it, don't I?" He looked to his men for support. Ki caught Dan Fellows's eyes. The gunman looked decidedly uncomfortable. Maybe, Ki thought, he was beginning to see through the masquerade Dantley was putting on for his men. It was difficult to tell. The big man was silent, still calmly holding his gun at the ready, still alert, ready to fight for the brand.

"I don't know why you kill," Ki said. "I only know people have been killed, their lives interrupted. I know women have been tortured and frightened and murdered. I would like to think that all of this wasn't done purely for the sake of profit, but that is how it seems."

"I don't give a goddamn how it appears to you, you bastard!" Dantley exploded. "We know the truth of things. We know you work for that Starbuck company, the company that wants to cut out all the small ranchers, all the hard-working little people in the country. Hasn't the woman got enough! Has she got to own the whole world?"

Dantley, pleased with his own speech, leaned back in his rocker and locked his gnarled fingers together. Ki still managed to maintain his outward calm.

"There is a courthouse in Fort Collins and a local sheriff, Dantley. May I suggest that you have us delivered there and let the law take its course if you believe your charges are justified?"

"Sure," the rancher sneered, "and see the Starbuck money buy you out of it all with a dozen fancy lawyers or a bribe passed over to a judge? Hell with you, mister. We've got range justice out here. We take care of our own trouble."

There was no arguing with the man. Both he and Ki knew that he couldn't afford to let Rebecca and Ki live. The other had been just a show put on for whichever of his men might have qualms about a lynching.

"What about the woman?" Ki asked.

"What about her? She goes back to her father, naturally," Dantley answered.

"It would be kinder to hang me," Rebecca said, and Dan Fellows, startled, looked toward her as Dantley's face was suffused with blood.

"You don't know what you're talking about, girl. You've been unwell," Dantley said, trying to keep the anger out of his voice.

"Don't I? I have lived with my father all of my life," Rebecca said, "and I've watched him change from a decent, hard-working man into a grasping, devious and very dangerous thing. I don't pretend to know what made this happen, but it's too true—he has changed into a man I don't know, a man who will do *anything* to further his ambitions, and I wish to warn you, Dantley, if you are foolish enough to trust him, you, too, will pay a heavy price.

"As for being mad, I am not, although it seems sometimes that I must surely go mad if I continued to live with my father, whose life now consists of blood and sex and money."

Dantley seemed slightly jarred by this speech. Dan Fellows and Archie glanced at each other. The other cowhands, half-hidden in the shadows of the room, were still and silent as if they weren't there at all. They had nothing against lynching this cattle-rustling Chinaman who had killed their friends, but the woman was a different matter. She seemed sincere, and it was difficult for the most skeptical of them not to half-believe her.

Dantley shook his head as if in pity, though the gesture was transparent. "Crazy," he muttered. Then he lifted his eyes to his men. "Told you she was crazy, boys. Her father told me she thinks she's a witch. Better watch out for her

77

black magic, huh?'' The joke fell hollowly, and with an impatient movement of his hand, Dantley commanded, ''Lock the two of them up! Use the storeroom. I'll do a little thinking on this so as to be fair, but damn me if I don't think we're going to have us a little neck-dancing party come morning, and good riddance to the man, I say.''

No one agreed. No one disagreed. Ki and Rebecca were led off down the dark hallway as Dantley, rocking furiously in his chair, watched with his dead eye. Ki tried again. Speaking to Dan Fellows, he said:

''Look, don't you see something's wrong here, Fellows?''

''Maybe,'' the man said through tight lips.

''The law isn't far away. They're the ones to handle this, aren't they?''

''Maybe,'' Fellows said again. He continued to move straight ahead to a heavy door, where he inserted a key and swung the oak-and-strap-iron contrivance open on its black hinges.

''It's not that far to town. Someone could take us over there—under guard.''

''I hardly think anyone can do that, friend,'' Fellows said as he stepped back from the door. ''The boss has already made up his mind, it seems.''

''But if he's wrong . . .'' Rebecca said passionately.

''Then I guess it'll have to be on his soul,'' Dan Fellows said stubbornly. ''Me, I work for this outfit. I take the man's money—whatever he says is what goes. That's the way it is. Sorry. Step inside, will you? I'll have someone bring along some candles and blankets.''

There was no choice but to obey.

There was little inside the room, little but cold and darkness. In one corner was a pile of sacking and, along the walls, shelving with canned goods. A bin of potatoes, five feet across, took up almost all of another small wall. Ki expected little more. Flour, potatoes and coffee, beans and lard would be all the staples he could expect to find in a ranchhouse. Meat was freshly butchered every day, of course, and any man with special needs, with the tobacco habit or a sweet tooth, would be expected to provide his own.

The door opened again, and as one bearded guard with a rifle watched from the hallway, a second entered with blankets and two candles set in beaten brass holders. The blankets were dropped on the floor by the wary cowhand, the candles thrust at Ki, who accepted them and four proffered matches without comment. The cowboy backed from the room and the door was slammed shut, the bolt slipped.

Ki thumbed a match to life, lit both candles and stood in the center of the storeroom looking around him, his hands on his hips, his eyes alert and probing.

"I can't go back, Ki," Rebecca said, and she came to him, her body convulsing with emotion.

"You won't have to," Ki said, stroking her fine dark hair. "I'll promise you that."

She stepped back and half-spun away in frustration. "How can you make a promise like that! We're stuck here, aren't we? I know you're a fighting man, Ki, but what can any man do to get us out of this?"

"I'll find a way," he said very quietly. "Believe me, I will find a way. You won't go back to your father again."

She attempted a smile, but it fell away into a bitter expression accompanied by an outpouring of tears. She sagged onto the pile of sacking in the corner, her head buried in her hands, and began to sob.

Ki looked away, staring blankly at the walls of the solidly built storeroom. A man should not make such promises, he told himself. How *was* he going to get Rebecca away from these people and to safety? He had spoken from pride, from

79

emotion, but the logical side of his mind spoke more loudly now inside his skull.

There was no way out, none. Only death for Ki and something perhaps worse than death awaiting Rebecca. He turned and watched the burning candle send smoke up from its wavering wick, wax beginning to drip toward the holder as the night and time went by, the woman cried and hope ran out.

Chapter 10

He hovered over her like a dark and deadly nightmare, his eyes glittering in the firelight. When Jessica Starbuck had first opened her eyes he had been there, watching. His hair was wildly brushed, his long, black mustache curled, his mouth an intimidating straight line beneath it. He wore a black robe with a crimson lining and black boots with silver spurs on them.

His name, he said, was "Manning."

"What is happening here, what is this?" Jessie demanded.

"Now you're mine; now you're one of us," the warlock responded.

"The hell I am," Jessica Starbuck shot back, and the man briefly appeared amazed.

"You can't fight it. I have the power. You will see," Manning, confident again, said.

"You have the power to *what*?" Jessica sat up with difficulty. She was still wrapped in a blanket and she tore it away from her body. Manning hovered, leering. Beneath the blanket she was naked.

"My women have brought your clothes, little one," Manning said. "For now, have no fear. We will dress you. Later you will be happy to have me see you naked. You will beg for it."

"You smug bastard," Jessica spat. "The day I beg you for anything will be the day I die."

"This, too, is possible," the warlock answered.

Now from behind him Jessica saw three women in black move forward. She was in a small cave, she noticed, and through the arched entrance to it reddish light fell on the stone floor. The women, backlighted by the sun appeared to be nothing more than shadows as they came to her and dropped her clothing on the floor. They wore hoods above their dresses, and their faces, lost in darkness were pale, nearly skull-like.

"Dress!" Manning said imperiously. "Then we shall talk."

"The man I was with, Roger Travis. What has happened to him?" Jessica asked.

"He was left where he lay," Manning answered with a shrug. "Perhaps he is alive; perhaps not. It makes no difference."

"It makes no difference!" Jessie said incredulously. "Does anything make any difference to you, Manning?"

"Yes, but not the life of an enemy."

"And what am I?"

"An enemy," Manning said deliberately. "You are an enemy, Miss Starbuck."

He turned his back then and walked away, his cape flowing around him as he moved. He seemed like a man walking through a stage role to Jessica, but an actor who believed his part so deeply that he had become it.

The women around Jessica Starbuck seemed to believe it all as well. They did not bow before him, but they moved back, submissive and obedient.

Jessie threw the blanket aside in disgust and dressed quickly as the women watched her with vague interest. Buttoning her shirt, tugging on her jeans, she got to her feet to stamp her boots on and comb her honey-blond hair roughly with her fingers. The witches watched every movement. At least one of them held a weapon in her hand, and Jessica knew that all of them were ready to leap on her and tear her apart if she gave any indication of resistance to Manning's orders.

"What's the matter with you all?" Jessie asked. "Are you women or slaves?"

There was no answer except for a deep, faint growling sound in the throat of the tallest of the witches.

Jessica started toward the mouth of the cave, disgust and anger building in her. No hand reached out to stop her. Outside it was brilliant morning, the sunlight glinting on the face of the quietly rolling stream, tinting the upper branches of the pines with gold.

There was a ledge outside the cave that was twenty feet or so above the riverbed, and there stood Manning, the morning breeze off the mountains shifting his hair, drifting his cape around his narrow body.

In full sunlight he was only a man in his early fifties, with gray showing at the temples and in his mustache. A man who might have been a shopkeeper or a bank teller. The cape he wore seemed an actor's contrivance, nothing more. His face was pale and weary looking, hardly sinister. He turned toward Jessica slowly.

"You may as well give it up, Miss Starbuck," he said in a low, stony voice. "You see, I have won."

"Have you now?" Jessie asked, her temper flaring. No one would tell her she had been beaten at anything until they had put her into a coffin. "I don't think so."

"Don't doubt it. You have lost this game. You cannot look for help from any quarter."

"I have a friend . . ."

"Kiai?" Manning asked with a quick, nasty smile. "Yes,

I have done my homework and I know his name as I know yours. I would not expect any help from your protector. He, too, has been captured, Miss Starbuck.''

Before Jessie could get over that shock the man went on, ''You and I know the sheriff will not aid you. You and I know the army will not ride over the mountains and save you. You may as well admit you are beaten, for it is so, it is so.''

''And so,'' she asked, ''what will you do with me now? Kill me?''

''Of course not!'' Manning said quickly. ''That is preposterous. A complete waste of a good woman.''

Jessie felt a chill creep up her spine. Carefully she asked, ''What does that mean?''

''You will find out, Miss Starbuck,'' he said as his pale hand briefly brushed her hair. ''I assure you, you shall find out.''

Jessica stood frozen, looking out across the river toward the far mountains. She knew exactly what her position was, and it was bad, very bad. Roger Travis was, if not dead, at least badly injured. Ki, if what Manning said was true, was also a captive. That left her no hope at all for escaping from this madman.

''Ki,'' she said under her breath. ''Where are you?''

Ki was on the run.

It had been just before dawn when he made his escape from Carl Dantley's makeshift prison. Pacing as the candles burned low and Rebecca slept fitfully, he had lifted his eyes to the ceiling and realized suddenly what he was looking at.

Staggered rows of one-by-six-inch planking were nailed to the log runners, and above these was the sod roof Ki had seen earlier. His heart lifted a little as he dragged a keg of nails to him and stood up on it.

Sixteen-penny nails held the planks to the log cross-beams, and as he tested one of the boards, he found that it moved, the nails creaking. The sound seemed harsh and loud in the night, although Ki knew that the guard, half-dozing on the other side of the heavy door, could not have heard it. He looked again, convincing himself that only the few hastily driven nails and the weight of the sod above held the ceiling in place.

A sound in the hallway caused Ki's head to come around. He was poised, ready to leap softly from the keg at the first indication the windowless door would be swung open. But this time there was no sound of the bolt being slipped.

He returned his attention to the ceiling.

The nails, driven into green wood, had loosened as the planks dried. Placing his palms on the ceiling planks again, Ki tried a little more effort. Again there was a small creaking sound as the nails loosened a little more. Rebecca slept, but it was better now to have her awake so that she would make no inadvertent sound and would be ready to move instantly if Ki was successful. He crept to her bed, and with one hand poised above her mouth, he gently awakened her by rubbing her shoulder.

Her eyes popped open, frightened and yet defiant by candlelight. But in the next moment she recognized Ki and her eyes became questioning.

He bent low and, cupping his hand to her ear, whispered: "Be ready to move quickly. Get up and pull your boots on."

"What is it?" she asked. "Have you found a way out?"

"I don't know," he answered honestly. "It is possible."

Ki liked nothing about his idea. If he could move the planking, with its heavy sod, noiselessly and somehow get Rebecca up onto the roof, they would still be surrounded by hostile guns, stuck in the far-up mountains without horses and weapons.

85

Still it had to be tried. Ki knew full well what lay in store for them if they simply waited.

The woman was sitting up nervously, her hands clasped together almost in prayer as Ki again clambered up onto the keg and braced himself for the effort. He glanced toward the door once and then concentrated all of his attention on the task at hand.

Crouching, he bunched his thigh muscles and closed his eyes briefly in meditation. His arms were rigid, the muscles leaping with the strain as he uncoiled his legs and put all of his strength into the work. Again the creaking of nails loosening, a sound seemingly loud in the night, came. The planking lifted slightly. Perhaps an inch or so. Ki had to slack the tension of his body and take a few deep, calming breaths. Perspiration had begun to sheen on his forehead.

Again he braced himself and again he pushed upward, his face a mask of concentration, every ligament and muscle of his body strained to the limit of human tolerance.

The great weight above him loosened, and sod fell into the room, trickling into Ki's eyes. With vast effort he lifted the planking still higher and turned plank and sod, clearing a narrow strip in the ceiling through which he could see one hopefully blinking star.

Then he heard the iron bolt on the storeroom door being drawn, and he flung himself from the keg, landing on the sacking, dragging Rebecca down with him. He had no sooner hit the makeshift bed than the door opened and a guard with rifle and lantern entered.

He could not fail to see the hole in the ceiling, the small pile of sod on the floor, to feel the cold draft from outside, and Ki swore silently.

The guard hovered over them for a minute. Ki could smell the liquor and tobacco on him. Then, with a grunt, the man turned, went out of the room and bolted the door again as

Ki lay there sweating, his heart pounding, Rebecca trembling beneath his arm.

Quick as a cat Ki was from the bed and back on the keg. The second plank came free more easily, and in a minute he had a hole big enough for both of them to crawl through.

Ki turned, gestured for silence and patience, and then, gripping the edges of the hole, he drew himself up and onto the sod roof. Cold air rushed over his perspiration-soaked body as he went to his belly and turned to drop a helping hand down into the room.

Rebecca took the hand and was helped up onto the roof, where she lay wild-eyed beside Ki, watching his face for direction.

Ki gave her shoulder a brief, comforting squeeze and then crawled away, inching toward the edge of the roof. From somewhere below he could hear voices and the music of a mouth harp. To Ki's left, half-hidden beneath the pines, was a corral with two dozen or so horses in its confines. The horses, dozing now, stood with their heads down as two cowboys quietly talked, one of them bursting into laughter.

To the samurai's right was a crude bunkhouse, similarly hidden by trees. There, lights burned, and it seemed to be there that the harmonica music originated.

Ki pulled his head back tortoiselike, quickly. There was a guard below him. The man, rifle in hand, had rounded the corner to Ki's right. Bored, moving with a slogging step, he nevertheless was dangerous. He carried a Winchester repeater and without doubt was an experienced gun-hand.

Ki felt Rebecca's hand on his back and he motioned her away. A second guard appeared a few minutes later, moving slowly in the opposite direction. Carl Dantley, it seemed, was taking no chances.

Ki had to make a move and he knew it. Sooner or later the guards inside the house would return to check on the

87

prisoners again and find them gone. It had to be done now and be done silently.

He inched back and whispered to Rebecca, "When you see me leap, do not follow. Not until you see me motion you."

"Ki . . ." He put his hand over her worried mouth, kissed her forehead lightly and then returned to his watching, his body coiled, positioning himself as the first guard approached again.

Ki, rising to a crouch, waited until the man was beneath him and then leaped softly into space. His body fell with the grace of a falling leaf, but when his feet struck the gunman's head it was with the force of a sledgehammer, and the guard went silently to the earth to lie on his face.

There had not been a sound louder than that of the guard's Winchester falling to the soft earth. Now Ki picked up the rifle, glanced to the roof to make sure Rebecca had understood her instructions and went to the corner of the building, where he waited, listening to the approaching boots of the second guard.

The sleepy man rounded the corner and caught the edge of Ki's open hand against his throat. He went down in a heap, never knowing what had hit him.

Now Ki motioned to Rebecca, and she jumped from the roof, skirts flying. Ki broke her fall, but still it was too loud. He pressed her to the ground, his eyes searching the night to see if the action had raised an alert.

He saw nothing, only the pines weaving in the wind before the star-filled skies, the rounded hills rising to the high mountain peaks where snowcapped escarpments glimmered dully in starlight.

"All right," he whispered. "Now!"

Ki grabbed Rebecca's hand and towed her to the corner of the house. There he crouched, his searching gaze fixed on the corral where the two gunhands had been. If he and Rebecca were to have a chance of escape they would need horses.

He squeezed her hand and with a moment's hesitation started off toward the corral, the woman in black, nearly invisible in the night, following him as fast as her shorter legs would allow.

From behind them Ki heard a shout go up, and lanterns were lighted in the house. Their escape had been discovered, and soon the thunder guns would open up, filling the night with flame and blood.

Directly in front of Ki, one of the two men guarding the corral seemed to rise from the dark earth, and Ki saw him go for a holstered six-gun.

A leaping kick thudded into the cowhand's chest just above his heart, and he fell back, his Colt revolver sending a round into the air. Ki, landing gracefully, cursed. The shot would tell Dantley's men exactly where the escaped prisoners were, and the bunkhouse would empty of armed men intent on tracking down Kiai and his witch-woman.

The second guard came on the run, but in the darkness he could not make out Ki nor the woman in black. He took a *nakadate* punch in the center of his forehead and fell back staggering. A small groan escaped the gunman's lips as he hit the ground, but that was all the sound he made.

No matter. The other cowboys were streaming across the meadow toward Ki and Rebecca. The door to the big house had been flung open, and light from within flooded the ground as Ki grabbed Rebecca's hand and dragged her toward the nearest of the horses.

As she mounted a dun pony, Ki grabbed the mane of a roan, taking only enough time to kick down the top rail of the corral. Then he began shouting, riding the confused roan in a tight circle, and the horses bolted from the corral directly

89

into the path of the onrushing cowboys, who had no choice but to scatter as the herd pounded toward them.

In minutes Ki and Rebecca were riding into timber, the stampeding herd falling behind, scattering as an occasional, random shot from behind sang through the trees, none of them near.

Then the night was quiet again, the forest empty, dark, and Ki slowed his hand-guided mount, and with Rebecca beside him, he aimed the horse toward Fort Collins.

Only at long intervals did they hear any sound behind them—the cowboys would be some time rounding up their horses and saddling them. By the time they were organized, Ki hoped, he and Rebecca would be too near to Collins for Dantley to risk pursuit.

Only occasionally, then, did they hear any sound from the long valley.

And only occasionally did they hear the weird moanings of the witches on the hilltops.

Chapter 11

The doctor was a small man with a red mustache, large freckled hands and a constantly worried expression on his narrow face. Now he looked deeply worried as he hovered over his patient, who lay on his back in the small room off the doctor's office. His head swung back and forth as he turned toward Ki and, nodding toward the patient with the bandaged head, said, "I don't know if he'll come out of this or not, to tell you the truth. The rock he was hit with was harder than his skull."

"Is it fractured?" Ki asked.

"No," the doctor answered, leaving the lantern in the room burning as he led Ki out to the office, where Rebecca sat on the hard wooden bench, hands clasped, waiting. "But the brain has taken a terrible jolt. It's about the same as being kicked in the head by a horse."

The doctor rolled his sleeves down and sat in his squeaking wooden swivel chair. Through the partially open door, Ki could still see the inert form of Lieutenant Roger Travis.

"He hasn't so much as moved since they brought him in," the doctor went on, "and that's what worries me. You could say he's unconscious, but when unconsciousness lasts as long as his, well . . . a man in a coma can't feed himself, and sometimes I think that a coma is just a preliminary to the long, deep sleep that waits for all of us."

"You don't expect him to revive?" Rebecca asked. She looked exhausted, was, from the long ride over the mountains to Fort Collins, where Ki had found Jessica missing, Travis in the doctor's care.

"There's no telling with these things," the doctor answered. "In the morning he might snap out of it and be demanding breakfast. Or . . . he may sleep in that bed until we have to call the undertaker."

Ki looked away, staring out the window at the dark street. He had hoped and expected to find Jessica Starbuck and Travis both well, perhaps having come up with some sort of plan to end the strike and rid themselves of the witches and Manning's evil. Knowing now what was behind all of this, Ki thought that some solution could be offered. Perhaps Dantley would have been willing to sell his herd to Starbuck Enterprises at a hefty profit, withdraw his support from the warlock and let the Comstock Central roll on.

Now everything was in chaos.

"I will be at the hotel overnight," Ki told the doctor. "If there is a change in the lieutenant's condition, please have someone wake me. At any rate I shall be here in the morning to see how he is doing."

"I'll let you know," the doctor said, but his expression and tone of voice gave no indication that he expected any change at all.

The night was cold as Rebecca and Ki went out, and Ki looped an arm around the woman's shoulder, warming her just a little. The sheriff, Ki knew, would be asleep in the room at the jail, but he was going to be awakened. Things had gone too far. The lawman couldn't simply ignore the situation anymore.

Ki's knuckles fell heavily on the door at the sheriff's office. From the rear of the building they could hear the drunken moaning of some unfortunate cowboy. It was a long, long time before Ki's insistent pounding brought the sheriff himself to the door, rubbing his eye with a knuckle while his right hand cradled a .44 Colt revolver.

"What in the hell do you want?" he demanded.

"Just the opportunity to talk," Ki replied.

"I've had just about all the talking with you people I want," the sheriff said. His eyes blearily roved over Rebecca Manning and then went back to Ki's face. "The hell with it—all right," he grumbled, swinging the door wide so that Ki and the witch could enter the dark office.

It was still warm inside; the iron stove still glowed dully. The sheriff tucked his revolver in his belt and crouched to prod the embers into brief life. Small, flickering flames showed inside the potbelly and then were shut out as the sheriff banged the stove door shut.

"Now, " he said, positioning himself behind his desk, revolver on the table, "what is it this time?"

"Attempted murder, kidnapping, assault," Ki said, not bothering to enumerate the many other charges a prosecutor could arrive at.

"If it's these damned witches you're talking about..." the sheriff began hostilely.

"Not this time," Ki said. "But this is all related. You see, Sheriff," he went on and explained all that had happened, as the sheriff, his eyes lowered, listened and watched the stove, where small flames burned behind the door grate.

When Ki was finally finished the sheriff just shook his head. "I still can't help you people," he said.

"Sheriff," Ki said, "I understood your reluctance before." He leaned forward in his chair, his eyes intent, hands clasped tightly. "Jessica Starbuck has been kidnapped. An army officer has been assaulted and may not live. These things happened in your town."

"Mister," the sheriff said mildly, but with strength. "I

93

don't know what in hell happened. A man got himself knocked in the head. He was sharing that room with your Miss Starbuck, the way I hear it. Far's I know she got into a quarrel with him, hit him over the head and took off."

"You couldn't say that if you knew Jessica," Ki said, growing angry now.

"But I don't know her. I don't know anything, you see," the sheriff said, seeming to find some satisfaction in that attitude. He leaned back, lacing his fingers together over his belly.

"You know what I've told you!" Rebecca said, her anger flaring suddenly.

"All I know is you took off from your daddy." The sheriff let his chair snap forward. "You took off from home, you been riding the mountains with this man. Maybe you feel like you have to invent a bunch of wild tales so that you won't get in trouble. Maybe you heard a lot of stories about witches and all so that you decided to tell me and everybody else that your daddy was whatever you call 'em, a warlock—I don't know."

The sheriff asked directly, "Are you a witch, girl?"

Rebecca looked at her hands, glanced at Ki and then sat staring at the floor as the soft glow of the dying fire highlighted her hair and carved deep shadow into the hollows of her cheeks.

"No," she told the lawman, "I am not a witch."

The sheriff shrugged. "Well then?" he said as if he had proven his point logically. Ki was smoldering with anger, but he could see there was no point in arguing further. All the sheriff wanted to do was be as uninvolved as possible, to remain by his fire and stay out of the cold mountains. There was no point in continuing the conversation.

Ki took the lady on a brief detour as they returned to the hotel. On the way up the street, she appeared puzzled and then merely concerned. Finally she asked, "What are you going to do now, Kiai?"

"What must be done," he answered with a shrug.

"Do I understand you?" she asked, pausing on the dark street to grip both of his arms and look up into his face.

"I think you do, yes."

"You're going back into the mountains. Oh, Ki, don't do that!"

"If you think I would leave Jessica Starbuck up there . . ."
She squeezed his arms again and then let her hands fall away.

"I know you wouldn't. I know that." She looked around them, her resignation turning to puzzlement. "What are we doing in this part of town, Ki?"

"I must take care of Jessica, but I will not let you feel threatened either," the *te* master said. "Come along."

It took Ki no time at all to find the men he wanted. Times were hard in the mountains and there were many hungry men. He had talked to one of these two before, and now he approached them with his proposition.

"I need two men to stand guard over this woman." He nodded toward Rebecca. "Twenty dollars a night between the two of you until I return."

"What's the catch?" the big Welshman named Gwynne asked.

"There's no catch at all so long as you do what is expected," Ki answered, and he saw the men's eyes light eagerly. "All I want is for you to watch her as she sleeps, a man in the hallway of the hotel, another outside her window. In the mornings if she goes shopping or out to eat, you will be there, a few steps behind.

"Decide between you when you each shall eat or do whatever you must do, but do not leave the woman unguarded."

"Someone's likely to come after her then," the other man commented.

"If it were not so," Ki said honestly, "I would not hire men to watch her. Yes, it is dangerous. But the ten dollars a night is yours for facing whatever might come."

The smaller man wore a long mustache which he now chewed thoughtfully. He glanced at Gwynne and the bigger man nodded—winter was coming and they were brutally poor. The pay was good and the danger in a town the size of Fort Collins seemed to be small.

"Sure," Gwynne said finally. "We'll watch her. You don't have to worry about a thing. Let me get my scattergun and I'll be at the hotel in fifteen minutes."

The smaller man said, "We wouldn't mind seeing some money now."

Ki agreed that it was a reasonable request, and he handed over sixty dollars, which were pocketed eagerly. Then, with Rebecca on his arm, he walked back to the hotel. She was very silent, gripping his forearm tightly. Outside the hotel she stopped him to ask, "Ki, will you be back?"

"Of course."

"How can you be sure—up there?"

"No one can ever be sure," the *te* master said. "But I will be back. Within three days." He smiled crookedly. "I must pay your watchdogs again by then, musn't I?"

The remark fell flat. Rebecca turned away and stared at the muddy, crooked streets of Collins. When she turned back her face had brightened with a false smile. "I know you will be back Ki," she said.

"Of course." Quietly he slipped her a pair of double-eagles. "Black doesn't suit you," he told her. "Buy yourself a new dress or two."

"Ki, you don't have to do this," she said, her emotions breaking through, so that her voice trembled and she stood looking down at the coins in her hand. "I didn't . . . I wasn't with you so that you would feel compelled to help me out."

"Woman," Ki said sharply, "if I believed that were so *I* would not have been with you, and I would not now be trying to continue to help you. Be silent now. You must eat and rest." He looked up to see Gwynne and his friend coming toward them, both of them armed with shotguns now. "I leave you in the hands of these men."

"But you will return, Ki?" she asked plaintively.

"I will return. It will be," he promised her.

And when the woman had been secured in her room and Ki was satisfied with the arrangements Gwynne and the other Welshman had made for her protection, he walked to the stable and hired a horse, a fine strapping black, and while the moon rose he started his ride back into the mountains where the witches roamed and the warlock held Jessica Starbuck prisoner.

The moon was half-full and the night so cold that the grass crackled under the horse's hooves. In the coat Ki now wore were *shuriken* taken from his bag at the hotel, and at his horse's side a Winchester .44–40 repeater.

Ahead, somewhere among the moon-silhouetted mountains, Jessica Starbuck slept or lay awake, a terrified prisoner of the madman Manning, hoping, and perhaps praying that Ki—the only one who could care enough to help her now that Travis had been injured—had somehow broken free of his captors, was somehow on his way to save her.

As she must have been hoping that somehow he would find a way to help her, so Ki wished that it would be so. He was a man alone against the coven of witches and Dantley's hired guns. Yet what else could he do but try to rescue her?

What else could he do, yet how could it be done?

Ki rode alone and the night grew colder, the stars grew brighter and his heart hardened to the impossible task.

Chapter 12

Ki rode through the night into the high mountains, the horse plodding steadily onward, new clouds from the north folding over the sky, threatening more bluster and rain. It was a cold, brooding night. Ki felt as frustrated as he had felt for years. There was no hint of help on any horizon. Their hope of ever resolving the timberland strike seemed as remote as the single cold star shining dimly through a rent in the gathering clouds.

But he found himself not caring about the railroad or the timbermen at all just then. His concern was immediate and much more personal.

Jessica had to be rescued at any cost.

He had seen Manning's work before. He had seen what the warlock had done to his own daughter and to the wife of Grange, the Welsh lumberjack. Nothing like that must be allowed to happen to Jessie.

Ki knew *they* were around him.

The Utes had been watching him, following him for miles now. What Nataka's people could want he could not guess. But it was their land, and they watched everyone who came and went, especially these nights.

Ki ignored the watchers in the woods and rode on, his destination the caves upriver where on this night Manning would be serving his Dark Master, where the witches would whirl and chant and—who knew?—perhaps prepare for a human sacrifice.

Jessica sat beside the fire in the cavern, watching as the witches, all pale and slender as if they never ate or saw the sunlight, sat in tight circles near her.

Some of them had tattooed pentagrams on their faces; others sat nearly naked, chanting and moaning indecipherable sounds. Somewhere outside the mouth of the cave Manning was speaking with another man. The other one wore range clothes, was gaunt and tall. His eye was peculiarly lusterless. Now and then a word drifted to Jessica, a broken phrase.

"Caught him with your daughter . . . somehow got out of there."

"How! Can't you do anything right, damn it!"

"Listen, Manning . . . slippery one . . ."

"Should've shot him on sight . . ."

Then the two angry men wandered out of her range of hearing, and Jessica was left to sit among the weirdly swaying, strangely chanting women, watching the dull glow of the fire.

Jessica wasn't feeling sorry for herself. She wasn't built that way. There was strong blood flowing through her veins. She was concerned about Ki, but relieved—she was convinced it was Ki they had been talking about outside. He was safe then, for the time being. What she had to do was find some way of making an escape without relying on Ki or on Travis. She had no way of knowing if Travis was alive, dead, injured or had simply given up.

Ki, she knew, would not give up.

But he could walk into something he could not handle. A dozen men with guns—for Manning and the other man had been talking about bringing in more gunhands; and if they knew Ki at all, they would know that he would not stop until he had freed Jessica Starbuck.

The way to keep Ki out of harm's way was for Jessica to escape on her own. She sat like one docile and afraid, her mind searching for a plan that would enable her to do that.

The witches themselves posed no barrier. They were swaying still, muttering; they seemed a mindless mass, slow to move. Jessica had long ago decided that she could bolt for the cave mouth and be outside before any of them would even react to her movement.

But outside were the men with the guns, and they would be alert, ready to stop her with an arm and perhaps a bullet, depending on the instructions Manning had given.

Now she rose and stretched, and wandered, with seeming aimlessness, toward the cave mouth. The eyes of the women around her lifted. They all seemed to hold an animal glow in the firelight, but no one made a move to stop her.

Manning himself confronted her as she neared the opening, stepping in from out of the darkness to place his cape-clad figure in front of her.

"Going somewhere, Miss Starbuck?"

"I need some air."

"You aren't going outside," he said.

"I didn't intend to. I just wanted to get nearer to the fresh air," Jessica replied, her voice growing sharper. "I'm tired of breathing the smoky air in here, of listening to the groaning of these misfit women, breathing in their rank scent."

"Testy, aren't you?" Manning said. His voice was slurred but confident, his smile twisted and obnoxious.

"Yes. I imagine many women who have been beaten and kidnapped grow testy," Jessica snapped back.

Manning laughed. He could afford to. He was in total control of things right then. He stretched out a hand toward

Jessica's hair, and she withdrew as if a rattler had struck at her. The warlock laughed again.

"You'll change your attitude in time," he said. "Once you figure out that your old world is gone and that I alone control your new one. That what I wish to give is given, that what I wish to withhold is withheld. That I have the power to make you comfortable or miserable, that I have the power over life and death, Miss Starbuck."

"I don't know if you're a charlatan or simply insane," Jessica said, and her voice was cold, as cold as the wind which drifted in through the cavern mouth and bent the flames of the fire. Glancing over her shoulder she could see the witches, their heads turned in unison, staring at her with empty eyes, their expressions angry and puzzled at once.

No one challenged the authority of the warlock.

"I am," Manning said with a heavy wink, "not insane, I assure you, Miss Starbuck."

"I will ask you once," Jessica said. "Let me go before this gets worse for you, much worse."

"Worse! No," he said, shaking his head, "it will only get better for me, Miss Starbuck. I have set my goals and now they are within reach. I have won, you see," he added complacently.

"Won what? What is it you want, Manning? Only to destroy lives and wreck honest efforts? I don't understand you at all, I really don't."

"Of course you do, Miss Starbuck," Manning said, his voice suddenly rising so that the witches all tensed and braced themselves for whatever was to come. "If anyone does, you do." He was panting into her face, and now his fingers, gripping her shoulders, dug in so deeply that it seemed they would go through flesh and nerves to her bones.

He slackened his grip slightly. His face was hawkish as he stepped back a little. His voice trembled.

"It's all profit in this world, isn't it, Miss *Starbuck*? If you don't understand that, no one does. Isn't that what your life and your father's life have been built around? Profit!"

"Honest profit," Jessica countered.

"Profit!" Manning shouted. "Whatever has to be done, it's only profit that counts. You wouldn't understand—you've never been poor. You've never had to live by your wits. You've never had to scheme and invent, convince, intimidate."

"No, and I never would, any more than my father did," Jessica said defiantly.

Manning began to pace before her, short tours that took him three steps to one side and three to the other, his eyes growing narrow and glassy.

"When you have money you don't understand what it means not to have it. It's all that matters. All! With money a man's a king; without it he's less than dog droppings. But you wouldn't understand any of this, would you?"

He turned suddenly and put his hands on Jessica's neck. She instantly thrust her hands inside of his and broke the grip, slapping the hands away. There was a communal groan from the witches and several of them rose to their feet. Jessica made a spur-of-the-moment decision, bolted beneath Manning's outstretched arms, dove for the mouth of the cave and in seconds was outside, a startled guard whirling, reaching for but missing her.

A rifle flashed flame from out of the darkness, the muzzle blaze seeming to light up the night like lightning. Jessica dove headlong over the rim of the bluff and went tumbling, rolling into the dark world below, where stone and earth pummeled her body as another gun was fired distantly, its discharge echoing in Jessica's ears as she tumbled through space and time. A rocky outcropping loomed up out of the darkness and struck her on the head, and as the guns splashed flame against the night, she continued to fall, her senses misting away until all that was left was darkness and insensibility.

Ki saw the rifles fire, and he leaped from the back of his horse to weave his way through the willow brush in the river bottom, leaving the horse ground-hitched.

He looked up and saw the crowd of black-clad figures surge toward the lip of the cliff shelf, and he darted that way, stumbling once in the darkness.

He heard a small moan and spun to see Jessica Starbuck on her face against the sand of the riverbed. He snatched her up to throw her over his shoulder as the guns continued their rapid random fire from above.

The witches were swarming toward them through the night. Some of them used the dim trail that led to the cave; others simply flung themselves from the bluff as Manning exhorted them with loud curses and sharp commands. Ki jogged on, Jessica inert across his shoulder.

Reaching the horse, he unsheathed the Winchester .44–40 and, placing Jessica gently on the ground, opened fire into the night, firing at any target offering itself, knowing that anything that moved on this night was the enemy, those who meant to hurt Jessica.

With his magazine empty, Ki finally paused, listening, watching. The night was utterly silent as the sounds of his own rifle firing quit ringing in his ears. It was as if he stood in an empty land alone. Manning had recalled his witches.

"What in blazes . . . ?" Jessica was sitting up, rubbing her head, and Ki wasted no time pulling her to her feet, swinging her up onto the horse's back and mounting behind her. He heeled the horse roughly, and the black leaped into motion, moving out with a fine, silky stride toward Fort Collins.

Jessica was still woozy when she turned her head toward

103

Ki and stared at him blankly. It suddenly occurred to her who she was with, that she was riding to freedom, that the long-striding black horse was Ki's.

"Took your time, didn't you?" she said. She attempted a laugh but it ended in a strange little coughing cry.

"Are you all right?" Ki asked, slowing the black horse to a trot as they reached an open meadow. The moon was rising now, glossing the frosted grass with silver.

"Yes. He's crazy, Ki, you know that, don't you?"

"Manning," Ki said grimly, "yes, I know he is."

"Travis . . . ?"

"He was not doing well," Ki told her honestly. "The doctor doesn't know what to expect."

"Damn them all," Jessica said softly. "If I had known, Ki, I would have brought an army of men in with us."

"You couldn't have known. All we knew was that there was trouble at Game Trail Camp."

"And we've done nothing to solve it yet," she said, her frustration breaking free. "Nothing except get Travis hurt, alienate the sheriff and waste our time."

"We shall accomplish something, Jessica. We will find a way. At least one of these young women is free of Manning's influence."

"Which one?" Jessica asked, not understanding.

"His daughter."

Ki went on to tell her about Rebecca and their capture and escape from Dantley, to explain exactly what lay behind the apparently pointless machinations of the warlock. Finally Jessie nodded her head in understanding.

"It's Carl Dantley that I saw tonight then. It's so simple, isn't it, once you understand it all."

"The question remains, what can we do to solve this, Jessica? The army won't wait much longer to lay in winter

104

supplies, and we won't be able to supply them with the beef they need."

"The question remains," Jessica said meditatively. She had no immediate solution to offer. For now, exhausted and still feeling battered, she was content to lean back and let Ki guide the big black horse back toward Fort Collins, where food and a bed awaited.

The first stop in Collins was the doctor's office. Cranky over being awakened at night, he nevertheless let them in, and the news he had was good.

" The young man sat up today and took nourishment. Other than complaining of a headache, he seemed to be feeling well. I gave him a sleeping powder and sent him off to bed again. He kept insisting he had to go find someone named Jessica—that's you, I assume, young lady."

"Yes. He's still asleep then?"

"He should sleep for another good four or five hours. Then, if all goes as it seems to, he'll simply be able to tug his boots on and go home."

"Can I see him?" Jessica asked.

"But I just told you he's sleeping," the doctor protested.

"I know that. I just want to peek in if it's all right," she answered.

"All right, then," the sleepy-eyed doctor replied. "Let me just make sure he's decently covered."

When Jessica was allowed into the room, Travis lay on his back, his hands folded peacefully across his abdomen. His blond hair was in a soft tangle, falling across his smooth forehead. He looked well; soft snoring rose from his nose.

"Glad to see you're all right, Roger," Jessica said, speaking softly, and it seemed that the army lieutenant smiled in his sleep. The doctor touched her shoulder and inclined his head, and they withdrew from the sickroom, the physician shutting the door quietly.

"Now then," he said, "if you two don't mind, I'd like to go back to sleep myself. I have a long ride out to the Calander ranch this morning to see to the croup their kid's got."

"Thank you," Jessica said. "We'll leave you alone. All I want myself right now is to sleep."

Outside it was very cold, the stars ice-blue, the street frosted. Having stabled up the horse, they trudged back across the crackling street to the hotel. Upstairs the miner named Gwynne sat with a shotgun across his lap before the room Rebecca was using. Jessica glanced questioningly at Ki.

"Manning's daughter, Rebecca," Ki explained shortly. "There wasn't time to talk about it on the way back."

There had been all the time in the world, Jessica reflected, but no matter. Apparently there was more to the story than he had wished to tell.

"For now, I suggest we both sleep . . . ." Ki's sentence was interrupted by the sudden opening of the door beside Gwynne's wooden chair. Rebecca appeared, blanket wrapped around her, smile curving her lips, eyes bright, and she rushed to Ki to embrace him with one arm while the other clasped the blanket together at her breasts.

"Kiai . . . I didn't think you'd be back."

"Of course I would be back," he said a little gruffly. There were tears in the woman's eyes, and he looked away, apparently embarrassed, although Ki was not an emotional man.

"I'm Jessica Starbuck, " the honey-blonde said, stepping forward. "Sorry I look a little the worse for wear. It's been a night."

"Can we talk?" Rebecca asked. "I know you must both be tired, but I can't sleep. I don't want to be alone."

"Sure." Jessica glanced at Ki, who nodded, and together, under Gwynne's eye, they entered the hotel room, where the lantern glowed feebly. Rebecca now turned it up so that the

106

smoky glow flooded the room with golden hues and deep shadows.

"I've been pacing the floor most of the night," Rebecca admitted as she sagged onto the swaybacked bed. "I was worried about Ki—and about you. I know my father too well."

Jessica was thinking other thoughts. She said to Ki in nearly a scolding tone of voice, "You haven't provided your lady with much Ki. You don't even have a nightgown or a robe?"

"No," Rebecca said, "but it's hardly Ki's fault."

"He should have thought of it anyway. I've got an extra robe next door—I'll get it. You can't have any clothes at all with you."

"I've only worn . . ." Rebecca looked at the black dress on the floor near the bed, her witch's garb, and Jessica shook her head with decisiveness.

"In the morning we'll get you some dresses. You'll not wear that in town, and with luck, you'll not wear it again— ever."

In a minute Jessica was back with a flowered flannel robe, and Ki was sent out of the room while Rebecca slipped into it. When he returned her dark hair was arranged. Jessica Starbuck, despite her own weariness, was finishing up with the brush and the hairpins she had brought.

Ki sat in a corner chair, somehow warmed by the sight. Outside the sun was approaching the horizon, the morning sky beginning to gray. He saw a flight of doves across the predawn gray, winging their way to their feeding grounds, and across town somewhere a baby bawled in anticipation of its morning meal.

Ki yawned once and then without realizing or meaning to, he fell into a deep and needed sleep.

He wouldn't have slept so soundly if he had known what was afoot in the mountains.

107

Chapter 13

Roger Travis reappeared the next morning. Stepping out into the bright sunlight, the young army officer winced as his eyes adjusted. Outside of a dull, throbbing headache, he felt fine physically, only a little wobbly at the knees. Psychologically he felt well also. The doctor had told him that Jessica had been to see him. That meant she must have found a way to escape the witches—or perhaps Ki had saved her. No matter, she was there in town and safe.

The day was brilliant, the sun beaming through scattered, high clouds that floated overhead and among the mountain peaks.

It was an effort for Travis to force himself to perform his duty first and put thoughts of Jessica in abeyance, but that is what he did, walking to the telegraph office, where the little clerk with the wispy white hair glanced up and smiled toothlessly.

"Thought you'd got lost, Lieutenant Travis. I sent a boy over to the hotel, but they said they hadn't seen you for a while."

"Why were you looking for me?" the blond lieutenant asked. "Has a message come in?"

"Yes, sir, it has. From your colonel at Fort Vasquez. I've been holding it for you."

The yellow telegram held a terse but explicit message for Roger Travis:

Lt. Roger Travis, Fort Collins, Colorado
Fm: Colonel Horace Beecher, Commanding Officer, Fort Vasquez.
Lt. Travis:
You are instructed to consummate agreement with Starbuck Enterprises within forty-eight hours or return to your post if this cannot be accomplished. Have made secondary agreement with local rancher named Dantley to deliver needed winter provisions.

Travis sent an answering telegram saying nothing more than that he had received the message and understood it. Then, thanking the telegrapher, leaving him a silver dollar as a tip, Travis folded the telegram from Beecher and went out again into the sunlight, which now seemed harsh and glaring.

He found Ki alone in the dining room at the hotel, sipping at tea, nibbling at dry toast while he watched the weather and passing parade outside his window. Travis walked to him and took an opposite chair, waving a waitress away.

"Jessica sleeping still?" Travis asked, removing his hat so that Ki was able to see some of the damage left by the stone. A lump, its surface scabbed, peeked out of the blond thicket of the army officer's hair.

"She took Rebecca shopping," Ki said with a smile. He explained it all briefly while Travis, his face concerned, listened. "She decided that a woman needs more than one black dress to get along."

"Ki," Travis asked, leaning forward intently, "what are we going to do? For myself, I'm running out of time." He handed the telegram over to Ki, who scanned it and passed it back across the table. "You see how it is. I'm going to have to pull out on you two if something isn't accomplished quickly."

"And as soon as you've returned to Vasquez and reported, Jessica's lost."

"That's right, I'm afraid. If there was anything at all I could do about it, Kiai, I would, but my hands are tied. You see that."

"All we can do then is take immediate action," Ki said contemplatively. Travis just sat and stared at the *te* master.

"Action? What sort of action, Ki?"

"I have several ideas," Ki answered. "They seem fantastic even to me, but when there is no simple solution to a problem, one begins to dabble with the fantastic."

"If only," Travis said, thinking out loud, "Carl Dantley had committed some provable crime."

"Even then the sheriff wouldn't act, would he? No, I'm afraid I'm going to have to attempt something even more drastic. Something not quite legal," Ki replied with another soft smile.

"I don't know what you're thinking of, Ki," Travis answered soldily, "but you can count on me to help out. I'll not leave Jessica in the lurch if I can help it."

"I'll do this alone," Ki said. "First of all, I don't think you're in shape for it just yet. Secondly, I work better alone."

"You won't tell me what you're thinking of doing?"

"Not just yet. Let's just say *they* have already tried it. Now it's my turn."

That did nothing to clear up Travis's puzzlement, but the light rapping of knuckles on the window beside them turned his head, and the sight of Jessica Starbuck, hair freshly brushed, face shining, temporarily drove the questions he meant to ask Ki from his mind.

The women waved and then disappeared briefly as they

made their way around the corner to the front door. When they reappeared Travis got his first real view of Rebecca Manning. Slender, with full breasts, she wore a flowered blue dress with lace at the collar and wrists. Her dark hair had been pinned up on top of her finely shaped skull, not ornately styled, but simply and tastefully done. She had a dab of rouge on her lips, it seemed, and her cheeks were heightened by natural color. In her hands she nervously clutched a small blue bag.

Both men rose and held out chairs for the ladies. Rebecca sat near to Ki, and now and then her hand would nervously stretch out toward his, not quite managing to touch it.

The witch was hesitant, but when Jessica insisted that she eat and ordered breakfast for her, Rebecca put it down ravenously—eggs, ham, potatoes and toast. Ki watched her indulgently and continued to sip at tea.

"Ki has some kind of plan to solve things," Roger Travis said to Jessica, "but he won't let me in on it for some reason." This came after Jessie, too, had seen the telegram and worriedly read it.

"Is this true, Kiai?" she asked.

"I have thoughts on the matter," Ki answered. Jessica knew him well enough to realize that he simply didn't want to discuss it in front of the others or near other ears in the restaurant.

"Let's hope your thoughts are helpful," Jessica said simply. Then she finished her coffee and leaned back, feeling futile suddenly. She watched the clouds scud past, listened to the dronelike chatter around her and now and then, with some impatience, glanced at Ki.

When Rebecca had finished eating, Ki left money on the table, and the four of them went out of the dining room. Jessica could see why Ki was withholding any plan of action from Roger Travis. The man would insist on being helpful,

111

and even Jessica could see that he still moved a little stiffly, that he was suffering pain and slight disorienatation from the blow on his head.

Jessica suggested that Travis escort Rebecca to the dressmaker's, where some simple alterations were to have been performed, and it worked well enough, so that Jessie and Ki were able to be alone in her room.

"All right, Ki," she said, "what's up?"

Ki closed the door and gave her a direct answer, "I am going to kidnap Manning," Ki said.

That took a moment to sink in. Jessica didn't gape, but her mouth screwed up in a thoughtful expression. If anyone could pull off such a bold plan, it was Ki, but still she knew how crazily hazardous it would be to attempt to capture the warlock.

"Are you sure, Ki?"

"I can think of nothing else. It is time to attack, Jessica, and the place to attack a body of evil is at its head, is it not?"

Jessica nodded and sat on the bed, her hands folded, her eyes on Ki. He was dead serious, she knew; and she saw a second reason Ki hadn't wanted Travis along. Ki was a cat in the night, a silent fighter. Possibly he could approach Manning's camp and perform this feat alone—at least he would have a chance. But not many men were mere shadows moving through the forest. Roger Travis was a warrior, a brave man and a confident one, but he simply didn't have the *ninja* skills necessary for this type of work.

"I don't like it, Ki," Jessica said, and Ki knew that Jessica realized exactly how dangerous this would prove to be, but she would not try to argue him out of it, not if he had his mind made up. She merely stepped to him, gave him one quick hug and said, "Watch yourself. Even the railroad isn't worth the risk of losing you, and you know it."

Ki just smiled briefly and promised to be careful—a somewhat ironic promise considering what he propsed to do. Then he returned to his own room to prepare himself, to take more *shuriken* from his valise and his curved knife from its compartment in his suitcase.

It was too soon still, he decided as he looked out the window. There were too many eyes out there. It would have to be later, as the sun faded out beyond the mountains. For now he would sleep as much as possible. He would need all the rest he could get.

When the sun went down he would hunt the warlock.

Dan Fellows sat with his bootheels hooked onto the middle rail of the corral, whittling as Archie squatted on the ground nearby. Both men were growing tired of the routine they had fallen into. The small man yawned, tilted back his hat and turned to look up into the sunlight at Fellows.

"I don't understand this kinda work, Dan."

"Whatever the boss wants," the always agreeable Fellows answered.

"Yeah, but," Archie said, plucking out a few grass blades from the base of the corral post, "we hired on to work cattle, Dan. True enough, he told us there might be some gunwork involved—that's all right, you and me saw plenty of that down on the Nueces—but so far's as I can see there ain't no one around trying to pick a fight or take the herd."

"There's been trouble," Dan said, but he said it without real conviction. Archie was right, and Dan Fellows knew it deep in his heart. This was a strange sort of outfit to be working for, like nothing he had known in Texas.

"So far all I've seen is a Chinaman and a girl," Archie persisted, standing up to face his friend. "Indians ain't bothered the beef. Ain't no other spreads around near."

"The boss says the railroad lady's out to cut his throat," Fellows said stubbornly if uncertainly.

"Yeah—that train ain't even runnin', Dan. How the hell they going to bring any railroad toughs up here?" Archie swung his head around toward the river country, where the caves stood along the bluffs. "You ask me, that's where the real trouble comes from. That Manning . . ." Archie fell silent as Carl Dantley emerged from the house and whistled sharply at them.

"Saddle my blue roan!" Dantley called, and Archie walked to where the boss's saddle and blanket perched on the corral rail. He slipped under a bar to catch the big roan.

Dan Fellows watched his friend grab the roan's bridle and lead the horse to the corral post, where he hitched it as he saddled up for Dantley. Then he looked back to the low, sod-roofed log house and shook his head. He began his aimless whittling again, keeping his head down as Dantley crossed the hard-packed yard to the corral.

"Going upriver," Dantley muttered as Archie led the roan out and held it until the boss swung into leather. That was all he said and neither of the Texas cowboys answered as Dantley spurred his big horse and took off at a gallop for the timber.

Archie looked at Dan Fellows one more time and said, "I think we ought to be riding home, Dan." Then he walked slowly off in his bowlegged gait toward the bunkhouse, where coffee was boiling.

Dan Fellows watched him for a minute and then returned to his tuneless whistling and whittling, only occasionally lifting his eyes toward the timber beyond the meadowlands and the river country beyond.

Dantley, meanwhile, wove through the coolness of the timber, cursing under his breath as he crested the piney knoll

114

and headed the blue roan toward the river. Manning was getting to be a problem.

He had sent a man over that morning with a note telling the rancher to meet him in his home camp near the caves. The tone of the note had annoyed Dantley more than anything. This Manning had damn near ordered the rancher to show up. Dantley, another Texan, was used to being in total charge of his people and intimidating those around him who weren't on the payroll. Now this Easterner with the black cape and strange ways had decided he was in charge of the proposition to take cattle through to Vasquez, that if it weren't for him, Dantley would sit there helplessly with his herd until they froze on their feet in the winter winds of Colorado.

Dantley growled as the two men rode out of the pine and cedar forest to flank him. Both of them were swarthy with full black beards. Crowley and Flynn were their names. They were Manning's men.

Where he had picked them up, Carl Dantley had no idea, but they were both known men, wanted in Texas and New Mexico for a little dirty work. Manning must have been paying them well—with gold . . . and with the women.

"You're kinda late, Dantley," Flynn said. He was a big man, built along the lines of Dan Fellows, but with none of Fellows's simple honesty, none of his honest courage. He wore a yellow rain slicker although it didn't look like rain and the morning had been dry. He favored a shotgun in his work, Carl Dantley knew, and maybe that was the reason for the slicker.

Dantley bristled as Flynn spoke. He was used to being called *Mr.* Dantley on his range, and he considered this his range.

"Not much," the rancher muttered between his teeth.

"Come alone, did you?" Crowley asked without turning his head. Dantley didn't even bother to answer this weasel of a man. Outside of being one of the ugliest men Dantley had ever seen—with his twisted, narrow face, broad lips, broken nose and bent-over right ear—Crowley had no quality at all worth noting.

Except his willingness to kill.

Despite himself, Dantley almost felt pity for Manning's daughter just then. These were the types of men the warlock would give his slave women over to to keep them working for him. Dantley had once had a daughter. A horse had kicked her when she was ten, and she hadn't pulled through; but while she had been alive she had had everything Dantley could provide her with—a pony and sulky, collie dogs and silk dresses, birthday parties where the children came from as far as a hundred miles away to be entertained on the home ranch . . .

The Chinaman, Dantley decided, didn't matter. Nor did the Starbuck woman. There were things a man had to do. Another man standing in your way just might have to be eliminated, and now and then it might be that a woman had to be killed. But you don't use your own seed, you don't threaten your son or daughter. If Dantley had any moral conviction in the world, that was it: you don't use your own.

The sun was high by the time the three riders reached the camp along the river and from his hilltop aerie the caped warlock descended to meet Dantley.

The rancher's mouth tightened as he watched Manning approach. He again considered how much Manning resembled a Shakespearian actor who has come to believe his own role too strongly. Crowley and Flynn stood to one side holding the reins to the horses, seemingly unable to control the smirks Manning's arrival provoked.

"Finally," Manning said in a haughty tone. "I've been waiting for you, Dantley."

"I'm here," the cattleman said. "What is it you want?"

"You allowed my daughter to escape." Manning turned his face toward the cobalt-blue river. "I have decided you must help me recapture her."

Dantley stood in silence for a long minute before he answered. "How do you mean, Manning?"

"You know what I mean!" Manning said, whirling toward the rancher so that the crimson underside of his cape flared up around him; and not for the first time, Dantley saw the unhealthy, mad gleam in the warlock's eyes. "I mean to take Rebecca back. I don't care what it costs. I will do it!"

"And just how," Dantley asked slowly, "do you intend to do that, Manning?"

"How?" The eyes grew stranger yet. "It's very simple, isn't it? I mean for us to go into Fort Collins. I mean for us to find Rebecca and then wreak vengeance on those who gave her shelter.

"I mean," the warlock said, as his glittering eyes met Dantley's, "to destroy Fort Collins."

Chapter 14

The wind was shifting the trees around the low bluffs and scalloping the face of the slowly winding river. The wind seemed to be moaning, too, deep within the caverns above them, but Carl Dantley knew full well that the sound wasn't from the wind. Like a human calliope, muted and muffled by stone, many in the caves voiced a sort of song like none Dantley had ever heard, and even this hard-bitten rancher felt a chill like dozens of cold fingers moving down his spine.

"You're crazy," Dantley said before he could stop himself, and the warlock stiffened, his face becoming bitter, eyes turning cold as winter ice.

"What did you say!" Manning asked, and his breath hissed through his teeth. From the corner of his eye, Dantley saw Manning's two personal bodyguards turn their heads away as if they wouldn't be able to stop themselves from laughing.

There was nothing at all amusing about Manning or what he suggested—quite the contrary. The only entertaining thing about it was that what Manning had said was absolutely true, and only Manning did not know he was a lunatic.

"Look here," Dantley said quickly, trying to avoid a confrontation on Manning's territory, "I don't blame you a bit for wanting to teach these people a lesson, Manning, but the fact remains, you can't take on a whole town to make a point."

"I have a few trusted men," Manning answered, "and I have my witches. Also we have your cowhands. That is a large enough force."

"Wait a minute," Dantley began. No one was going to take his cowboys into Fort Collins to start a war. "I can't . . ."

Manning wasn't listening at all. "They won't fight," he said complacently. "Do you think the Welshmen or the Chinese will come out to do battle with my witches? I assure you they will not. Not because they are 'superstitious,' but because they know the true strength of the Dark Master, the power I have from him."

"Manning," Dantley tried again, becoming a little frightened despite himself, "it won't work."

"Why not? Is the sheriff going to stop us? The army? The citizens of Fort Collins?" The warlock shook his head. "No one can stop us so long as we work together."

"What in hell do you hope to gain from this?" Dantley half-shouted. "Outside of revenge against the Chinaman, what's to be gained?"

"That is enough to gain," Manning said, crossing his arms royally.

"For God's sake, man, what about the investment we've got wrapped up in getting this herd through to Vasquez? All we can do is bring trouble down on us and lose the damned investment."

"You are telling me you won't do this with me," Manning said, his voice flowing cold like the river.

Dantley shuddered a little. But the rancher was no coward, and he straightened up and said, "No! It don't make no sense, Manning. You want to take a bunch of women and storm a town filled with armed men. You want me to throw all my hands in on this wild-hare gamble. I can't go along with that.

119

Your thinking ain't straight, and you're going to ruin my scheme on top of it.''

"It is something that must be done," Manning said in the same imperial tone. Again he folded his arms, and Dantley spun around in disgust. Near him in a circle now, much closer than he would have believed they could have crept, was a group of twenty or so black-clad witches, stones and sticks in their hands.

Dantley's hand slid to his holster and came up filled with a .44 Colt. He took a step back and glanced at Manning. The warlock smiled smugly and spoke.

"There's no need for the gun, Dantley. Sisters! This time we shall let him travel away. This time we shall not tear him limb from limb and scatter his bones to the wild creatures. We may still have use for Mr. Dantley."

With a sound like the growling of a mass of feline creatures, the witches backed away as Dantley, his knees wobbly, walked to his horse and swung aboard, the insufferably smirking Crowley and Flynn with him.

Dantley snapped the roan's head around and splashed across the river, swearing all the way, the two gunhands flanking him as he rode.

He was fifty yards into timber before he slowed his horse and snapped at Flynn: "Are you two as crazy as he is? How in hell can you ride for a maniac like that!"

"He pays," Flynn answered mockingly.

"I wouldn't mind shifting over to your side," Crowley put in. "If you wanted to match his offer. Tell me, Dantley, what would you pay us?"

"Spit," the rancher answered, and Crowley reached for his handgun, but Flynn just laughed.

"Put it away, Crowley. It ain't worth it." Then he reined his own horse up, and as Crowley followed suit, they left

120

Carl Dantley to ride back to the ranch alone, muttering bloody curses all the way.

Manning, meanwhile, had made up his mind. He waited only until Crowley and Flynn returned. Then, standing on a low, river-pocked rock like a dark patriarch, he summoned his witches to him and, after a long, meandering speech about the power of the Dark Master, shouted to Flynn, "Break out the rifles. See that each woman has one. We are on our way to Collins. My daughter will be taken back. The one who stole her away will be killed. The blond woman who opposes me will be captured.

"Let no one stand in our way! We are martyrs for the cause no man can stand before!"

Crowley and Flynn dragged a case of repeating rifles from the cave behind Manning and loaded them as the witches, one by one, stepped up to take the weapons.

"I ain't no martyr for the cause," Crowley muttered, but Flynn silenced him with a finger across his lips.

Flynn was no martyr either, but there had to be a way to make all of this madness work to their logical advantage. He pondered that as the two of them continued to load the weapons and pass them out to the pale, obedient witches, as Manning continued to rant on, perhaps convincing himself of his own dark, invincible destiny.

"We'll just keep watch," Flynn said under his breath. "We'll just keep watch and see where this all might carry us if we play our cards right."

Minutes later they rode out toward Fort Collins—Manning on a black horse, blacker than night, without a white hair on its body, and behind him his army of witches, cowled, dressed in black, followed by Flynn and a nervous Crowley.

There's a long valley without a name where the White Badger Creek splits and over the eons has carved two valleys, north

121

and south, before joining again and flowing down to the South Platte. The land there is all timbered heavily, and the long island formed by the river stands majestically above the little river.

As Manning and his party of witches rode through the north valley, a lone warrior on a gray horse rode in the opposite direction up the south valley. Kiai, come looking for the warlock, passed Manning by without knowing it.

Collins, without knowing it, was awaiting the storming of the town by a company of armed and bloodthirsty witches.

Jessica Starbuck, in Fort Collins, stretched and yawned behind her hand and smiled at Lieutenant Roger Travis. The night was cold and clouding up again, but they had had a good steak-and-potatoes dinner in a warm restaurant and intended to use the cool of the evening as an excuse to warm each other's bodies. In the middle of all the madness, they could still give each other that much comfort.

Rebecca Manning, guarded still by her faithful Welshmen, slept deeply in the room across from the absent Ki's. Jessie worried about Ki, true, but the *te* master was capable of taking care of himself, and worrying would do no good. All she wished for now was a warm and loving night, a deep and fretless sleep and a brighter morning.

The town was quiet. The usual knots of Chinese and Welsh timbermen hung around the corners, many of them turning their heads away in shame as their employer walked past on the arm of the young army officer.

"It's hard not to feel sorry for them," Jessica commented as she clung to Travis's arm.

"They've dug their own hole," Travis answered.

"Not really. It's in their culture, the things they believe, the things they honor or fear."

"Philosophical tonight, are we?" Travis asked with a boyish grin.

122

"Too tired to be philosophical," Jessica answered. "Afraid I haven't quite caught up on my rest yet. All I feel like doing is resting—well, almost all—yet I feel like I should be doing *something* for the railroad."

"What's left to do?" Travis asked. "Nothing, nothing at all. And," he added, "there's nothing left to do for these men."

"And for you?" Jessica asked impishly, smiling up at the officer.

"There's always something you can do for me, Jessica Starbuck," he replied, looping his arm around her shoulders, squeezing her to him.

"Let's work on that then. It's better to work on something you can do something about than to worry about things you can't do anything about, isn't it?"

"So they say," Roger Travis answered.

For the most part the town was quiet as they made their way back toward the hotel. The cold was keeping those who had someplace to be at home. The saloons were quiet, too. Who among the timbermen had the money to drink away? Outside of a few cowhands from the small outlying ranches and a few bored, dingy women trapped between lost youth and imminent age, there was no one in the gin mills.

The hotel, too, was quiet. It was too late for supper, and those with any sense were curled up beneath their blankets and quilts, sleeping warmly. There was a bored desk clerk and an old man with shaking hands and a week-old Denver newspaper sitting in the lobby. Otherwise they saw no one as they made their way, arm in arm, to the stairs and ascended to their room.

That was when the explosion shattered the silence of the night.

It was sharp enough to shake the floor beneath Jessica's feet, sharp enough to bring Rebecca upright in her bed and

123

cause the Welshman, Gwynne, to leap from his wooden chair in the hallway and cock his shotgun, looking up and down the corridor as other residents of the hotel peered cautiously from their doors.

In his room in the jailhouse, the sheriff leaped from his bunk, figuring that some of the captured Frank Williams's gang had decided to blast him out of the brick jail and free him from the hangman's noose.

Jessica, after a brief moment's confused hesitation, rushed back to the door of the hotel, noting that the front window had been broken out by the explosion sending shards of glass to the floor.

In her hand was her Colt .38 and at her shoulder was Roger Travis. Looking up the street, they could see flames jutting from near or behind the dry-goods store.

A pair of riderless horses came thundering down the street, eyes wide in panic and confusion. They stepped on their reins with their forehoofs and stumbled before disappearing into the darkness south of town.

Then from uptown came the sound of rifle shots and an agonized scream. A second fire had started somewhere near the Red Dog Saloon.

As Jessica watched, her thumb on the hammer of her revolver, a swarm of dark-clothed figures flooded the streets of Fort Collins, debouching from the alleyways. More frightened horses pounded past and a woman screamed. Gunfire rattled the night and another explosion sounded from the distance.

The attack of the witches had begun.

Chapter 15

The dark mass of black-clad attackers flooded the main street of Fort Collins. An older man peering out from the hotel balcony took a .44 slug in the head and tumbled over to the street below to lie with his nightshirt tangled around him.

Jessica Starbuck herself had to jerk her head back from the window as she saw a witch raise her rifle and aim. As Jessie hit the floor, the bullet pierced glass and window frame, showering her with splinters of wood and glass.

She lifted up her head and triggered off two rapid shots from her .38, each of which missed its target as the witch took to her heels and fled up the street.

Uptown the fighting was intense. Jessica couldn't tell from her vantage point exactly what was going on, but there was heavy gunfire in the streets and from the windows of the business establishments along the muddy road as the fire blazed spectacularly behind the moving figures, sending fountains of red and gold flame into the Colorado skies.

She spun away from the window as she heard the gunshots ringing inside the hotel itself, heard the excited shouts of residents and the shrieks of the attacking witches.

Jessica made her way to the hall door where Travis had already positioned himself.

"Where are they?" he shouted, but Jessica could only shrug. The army officer crouched, looked back toward the front entrance to the hotel and then again to the outside hall door. Sounds, eerie and indefinable, drifted around them, punctuated by the distant shots from farther uptown.

Smoke now wafted even to the hotel lobby, from the conflagration begun by the witches—a fire, Jessica now realized, that had been intended only as a diversion while the witches rushed the hotel.

"It's Rebecca they'll be after," she said without a shadow of a doubt, and she ran past Travis's grasping hand toward the stairway leading up to the second-floor rooms, her revolver at the ready.

Above her the sudden boom of a shotgun roared, and she knew she had been right. It was Gwynne who had fired, and as Jessica, taking the steps three at a time, reached the upstairs corridor, she saw the stunned Welshman standing near a black-clad body. He turned a horrified face toward Jessica Starbuck.

"A woman . . . I've killed a woman," he said, awed at his own violent action.

"Damn it all, quit worrying about it and reload," Jessica Starbuck said sharply.

But she hadn't said it soon enough. The window at the end of the corridor was open, and Jessica saw the muzzle flash as a witch triggered a round through the barrel of a Winchester repeater. Gwynne staggered back, holding his face, the back of his head blown away.

The Welshman slumped to the carpet, his blood smearing it with dark gore as Jessica, from one knee, two-handed her .38 and the witch in the window was blown back to fall to the alley below, her scream fading as she tumbled.

"What is it!" Rebecca Manning appeared in the doorway to her room, her wrapper hastily hung from her shoulders. She caught sight of the dead bodyguard on the carpet and her hand went to her mouth.

126

Jessie shoved her back into the room roughly as another shot sang through the corridor from the window, ripping the paneling from the wall beside the door.

"Stay down!" Jessica yelled, and Rebecca obediently went to the floor as the glass burst from the window frame of her room and two witches tried to force their entrance through.

Jessica fired twice and saw one of the women twist away in agony. The other fired into the room sending Jessie herself to the floor.

She fired from her back as a witch stepped over the sill, rifle still in her hands, her lips curled back in a mad snarl. Jessie's bullet took the witch in the shoulder and slammed her back like the kick of a mule.

Hastily she reloaded. Rebecca was still, silent as death, but well. From uptown the gunfire continued and the flames burned hot enough for them to hear the crackle and snap in the hotel. The sky outside was alive with weaving color—crimson and hot gold.

In the next second the fire was even closer as a burning brand came flying through the window. Jessica dove for it, but before she could even reach it the curtains were going up in a sheet of flame. She reached over and grabbed Rebecca's hand, lifting her to her feet as the kerosene-soaked torch spread fire to the walls and bedding in less than a minute.

"Come on! Now!"

Yet another witch appeared in the window, her face a ghastly bone-white in the firelight. Jessica winged a shot at her and missed, but the head withdrew rapidly as she tugged Rebecca toward the hallway.

Outside they found Travis kneeling beside the body of one of the ugliest men Jessica had ever seen. None of them knew Crowley's name, but it didn't matter anymore. Rebecca gave a small shriek, a muted, strangled noise. Travis lifted his eyes.

"I don't know who in hell he was, but he drew down on me. I got lucky."

"We've got to get out of here," Jessica said. She nodded back toward the room where the fire still blazed, growing hotter. Up the hallway fire roared in another of the hotel's rooms.

"Yes," Travis said standing. "Where?"

"Let's get the hell out first and then decide," Jessica said. That might be more difficult than it sounded. The witches certainly would be watching all of the exits, and it was Rebecca they were undoubtedly looking for.

Down the corridor now the other hotel residents made their way through the smoke, many of them wearing dampened blankets around their heads. Jessica kicked open the door to an empty room and tossed Rebecca a blanket.

"Put it over your head," she ordered, and Rebecca obeyed. Jessica followed suit. With any luck it would keep them from being recognized for just long enough.

Travis led the way down the stairwell to the lobby. In the center of the room, the desk clerk lay, blood from his body staining the carpet.

Outside the skies were still fire-bright. As the hotel occupants tried to get outside, gunfire sparked. The witches were firing indiscriminately, but luckily with little success. Besides, most of the hotel's residents were armed themselves, and they returned the fire, keeping the snipers' heads down.

Travis stepped out onto the plank walk in front of the hotel and threw himself to one side as muzzle flashed in the alley across the street alerted him to the presence of more snipers. Bullets tore at the hotel wall behind him as Jessica and Rebecca, blankets over their heads, rushed out of the hotel under his covering return fire.

Then the three of them were away, into the alley behind the hotel, where a dead witch lay and past that to the railroad tracks, where the Comstock Central locomotive and its passenger cars sat before the depot platform.

Jessica's engineer and three other railroad employees, Jules Jenkins among them, were aboard, guarding the train with ready weapons.

"Thank God!" the station manager said as Jessica, shedding her blanket, reached the steps of a Pullman and was tugged aboard. "I was worried you were caught up in all of this, Miss Starbuck."

Jenkins still seemed more worried about losing his job and pleasing his boss than anything else, but it didn't matter. With the doors to the Pullmans closed and latched and the extra guns around them, she, Rebecca and Travis were relatively secure. But was that enough?

The town was burning swiftly now. A towering plume of smoke and fire rose above Collins's main street.

The Dark Master was having his night.

Jessica found the engineer, whose face was glistening with perspiration. His hands were wrapped so tightly around his rifle that his knuckles were white.

"Back the train out of here before the fire reaches us," Jessica said.

"We haven't got much wood or much water," the man said doubtfully.

"Just get us back down the tracks. A mile will do it. Get up a head of steam and move this rolling stock. No sense losing everything."

"Yes, Miss Starbuck," the engineer said, and he moved back toward the locomotive, apparently relieved to be back on a job he understood.

Peering out the windows of the dark Pullman, Jessica could see no sign of attack. She turned toward Travis.

"Stay with Rebecca, Roger, will you?"

"Wait a minute! Just what do you have in mind?"

"Finding the sheriff," Jessica Starbuck answered. "Someone has to get things coordinated here. These women are going to destroy the entire town if they're not driven off."

"Let me do it, Jessica," Travis pleaded. "It's no place for you—out there."

"It's no place for anyone," she said with a short smile. Then she kissed him, and before he could say another word, Jessica Starbuck had slipped out the door and was gone into the night.

Still the rifles crackled near the main street, but the reports were nearly drowned out by the fire storm that raged on relentlessly.

Jessica started up a dark alley near the feed store. The wall to her right was red with firelight, the wall to her left pitch black, cast in deep shadow.

From the shadows the witch rose. The combination of firelight and shadow made her face into a skull-like mask. She seemed to have no eyes at all, so deeply sunken were they. She shrieked something unintelligible and lunged at Jessica, a knife in her bony hand.

Jessica spun and side-kicked the knife from the woman's hand, hearing the sound of bone cracking. There was a following howl as the witch, holding her wrist, scuttled off toward the heart of town.

Main Street was madness. Blazing with red-orange fire, it was overrun with people. A fire brigade tried to fight the flames, which were threatening the hardware store and adjacent milliner's shop. Horses wandered aimlessly in the lower section of the street, having been turned from their hitching rails.

Gunfire still sounded, near and harsh. As Jessica watched, a man with a fire bucket went to the ground, spilling the precious water he had been carrying, to lie still and crumpled against the earth. She swore that she could hear a following cackling laugh above the roar and whip of the flames.

That might have been imagination, but it wasn't imagination that showed her the flitting, dark figures on the roof of the burning building. The witches, doomed if the fire was not put out, nevertheless stood on the roof above the fire fighters, as they tried to pump water through their hoses, and shot at them with repeating rifles.

Thank God they weren't marksmen, but they were good enough to kill occasionally, to prevent the less courageous of the fire fighters from attempting to save the building, which now glowed hotly through all of its lower-story windows, a gold and deep red glow like that of an ember. The heat was intense enough to drive Jessica back from her first attempt to cross the road. The few brave fire fighters continuing to work were soaked in sweat, darkened with ash, swearing, tugging at their equipment with brawny, fire-burned arms.

Jessica heard the creak and groan of the building, and as she looked up in horror, it collapsed, sending out waves of super-heated wind. And on the rooftop the witches fell into the flames of their self-created hell, shrieking and shouting male curses.

Jessica crossed the street and rushed on toward the sheriff's office.

Inside, the sheriff, his pipe in his mouth, was standing with three other men, hovering over a town plan. All of the men looked around sharply as Jessica entered. One of them, burly, fire-blackened, touched his hat. The others ignored her.

A rail-thin man with a red long-john shirt, badge affixed, stood nodding at every word the others spoke. An older man, face puffy and crimson with excitement, kept tapping the town plan.

131

"If the fire spreads to the courthouse, then we'll lose the school, too. And the Methodist church!"

"Yes, Your Honor, but we can't do a damn thing about it," the sheriff said. "We've got snipers on the rooftops and in the alleys. I can't send any more men out to try to soak down the courthouse. It's the same as a death sentence."

The burly man was apparently the volunteer fire department's chief. He said, "I've got as many people out there as I could round up, Mayor. But it's gotten too damn big—about all we can do at this point is hope it burns itself out by dawn."

"No," Jessica Starbuck said, and they again turned their heads in unison. "We can do one other thing—we can eliminate the snipers."

"Just how do you propose to do that, Miss Starbuck?" the sheriff asked. "Rooftop snipers in the darkness. It's as much suicide to try doing that as it is to try fighting the damned fire."

"This way you may at least save part of the town," Jessica pointed out. "Of course, if you had listened to us before . . ."

"Yes, yes," the sheriff said, cutting her off. The mayor glanced sharply at him, his eyebrows lifting. Obviously the sheriff didn't want to admit that he had known about the witches, been warned what they might do and ignored the situation.

The deputy stopped his nodding long enough to say, "The lady may be right. Go after them women."

"And who in hell are you going to find to shoot women?" the sheriff demanded.

Jessica didn't have to answer; the fire chief did it for her. "Anyone who wants to have a home in this town by morning," he said, and the mayor, his small mouth puckering, had to agree.

"I can try to get my people to help," Jessica said. "They

couldn't fight what they couldn't see, and they didn't see any reason to fight for the railroad at the risk of their lives. Maybe now, with their homes and their families' lives at stake, they'll come through.''

"I wouldn't count on it," the sheriff muttered. He still apparently considered the timber workers outsiders, cowards, and worse.

"I'm not counting on anything," Jessica said. "But we have to try, Sheriff." Her eyes went to the mayor, the fire chief and back. "We'd better try something or there won't be any Fort Collins come daybreak."

Chapter 16

What threats and wheedling couldn't accomplish, the sight of the jutting flames over Fort Collins did. Jessica had her timbermen enlisted in the fight to save the town within a matter of minutes. Chinese and armed Welshmen moved out into the streets, which blazed nearly as brightly as day, and there the twin battle began: the battle to save the town from flames and to drive the attacking witches away.

Jessie's contingent, made up of those who worked for her, were primarily concerned with the second task. Along with the sheriff and his lone deputy, they set out to rid the town of the dark menace of Manning's black-clad women.

The sheriff seemed befuddled or overwhelmed by the war taking place in his town. It was left to Jessica to organize the battle plan. She wished that Ki were there to take charge, but Ki wasn't, and so it was her task, and she felt up to it— how many battles had she been through, from the Mexican border to the Canadian, in deserts, mountains and even in the skies?

Yes, she was woman enough for the job.

The battle wasn't going to be an easy one. The witches had position. All of the main street was covered by rifle fire. Worst of all, the enemy Jessica faced had no fear of death apparently. They stood still before the flames and fired their weapons as the timbermen moved out of the meeting hall toward them.

A man beside Jessica went down almost immediately, clutching his leg. A friend dragged him into an alley where smoke lay in heavy wreaths.

The hotel had caught fire now, and Jessica drew herself up against the wall of the saddlery to shout at the sheriff above the roar of flames.

"We won't get them down from there unless we go inside the hotel and onto the roofs."

"You're crazy," the sheriff yelled back. "It's ready to go too!"

"We don't have any targets from here," she shouted back.

The sheriff swallowed hard and glanced behind him at the smoldering building. He was clenching his rifle so tightly that you would have thought he was trying to strangle the life out of it.

Across the street another man,—a Chinese, went down in agonizing pain as a bullet ripped through his shoulder, and the sheriff swallowed hard again.

"It's try the staircase to the roof or watch our people get cut down one by one on the streets," Jessica said firmly. She could see the thoughts behind the lawman's eyes—fear, uncertainty, doubt that a woman should tell him what course to take here.

But his town was burning and there was no option he could see. Finally he nodded.

"Lead on," the sheriff muttered.

Jessica was no happier about it than the sheriff was, but lead on she did. She kicked open the hotel door and slipped in, half-expecting to draw fire from the head of the first-floor stairs, but none came. As she covered the lobby with her .38 Colt, she waved the sheriff inside. His deputy and three Welshmen, all armed with Winchester repeaters, followed.

135

Jessica looked again at the sheriff, and it was immediately clear that whatever was to be accomplished here, it was up to her to take the lead.

She moved toward the stairs, her hat hanging from its drawstring, her Colt held level beside her waist. The sheriff tiptoed behind her, the angry Welshmen nearly pushing him along as they reached the stairs.

Smoke drifted through the lobby and wafted up the stairs, but there was none of that heated glow of flames as yet, only lanterns burning dimly in the upper corridor. Jessica moved upward slowly.

The witch appeared at the top of the stairs. She was naked, screaming something unintelligible, and in her hands was a shotgun. She triggered the scattergun at the same time Jessica's Colt banged out a shot. The shotgun sprayed the wall beside Jessie's head with birdshot, but the .38 did the real damage. The bullet ripped up through the witch's breast, and with a scream of agony, the woman toppled forward and over the balustrade, falling to the floor below.

The smoke was thicker upstairs, the air hotter as Jessica Starbuck led her warriors upward and forward. From the corner of her eye she caught a glimpse of a figure emerging from the door, and she hit the carpet, rolling to one side as a rifle spoke loudly in the close confines of the corridor and flame spat from the muzzle of a Winchester.

Jessica rolled to her back for a shot, but it wasn't necessary. One of the Welshmen yanked the trigger of his revolver and blew the witch back into her room.

With a savage curse the timberman shakily helped Jessie to her feet, his big calloused hand wrapping around hers.

"Never thought I'd shoot a woman."

"It was her or us," Jessica said.

"Them or the town," the deputy said with surprising determination. Even the sheriff looked resigned to the reality of things now—they would all have to kill some women if the town was to survive. Or were they women at all, these strange, twisted creatures, Jessie wondered, or just some semblance of human females Satan had spewed forth from his dark and tortured hell?

Manning. It was Manning she wanted to find.

Ki had mistakenly gone hunting the warlock in the hills, but he was here in Collins, exhorting his dark army on to still more destruction. He had to be found.

He had to be exterminated.

Cautiously Jessie moved along the hallway. At each door she paused, opened or kicked the door in and stepped to one side; but there were no more of the dark ladies hidden there.

From the rooftop they could still hear rifle fire, and now and then a shriek or curse or moan. Directly ahead of Jessica now was a ladder leading to a trap door and the roof above. The pale glow of flames showed through the rectangle cut into the ceiling, and in a second that was highlighted by the sharp colors of a muzzle flash as a witch, bending low, leering, cut loose with a pistol, spinning the deputy around as a .44 slug caught the flesh and bone of his shoulder.

As the deputy screamed out in pain, the sheriff, suddenly shaken out of his lethargy, fired back with his rifle, sending three shots from his Winchester into the open trapdoor, showering them all with splinters, dropping the witch to the floor of the corridor.

It was still Jessica who assumed the lead as they stormed the ladder and burst out onto the roof, where the flames seemed to burn as brightly as day and the strange, black-costumed women danced and howled and fired death through the muzzles of their rifles into the street below.

Jessie emerged onto the roof and went into a crouch as two rifles stabbed flame in her direction. She fired to the left and switched to the right almost instantaneously, the double-action Colt firing rapidly as if it had a will of its own.

One witch staggered back, hit the parapet and fell to the street below like a wounded crow sailing through the fire-lit sky. The second simply folded up into a black heap.

The sheriff, cursing loudly and frantically, hoisted Jessie to her feet. She could see the blood leaking from his shoulder near the base of the collarbone.

"Bitch tagged me," he was saying repeatedly, "damn it all, the bitch tagged me."

He, too, had apparently lost all of his inhibitions about shooting at women. To Jessica's mind it had never made a difference. She understood full well that these were frontier men, used to protecting their women, to doing the fighting for them, to perhaps investing them with a few better and more idealistic qualities than they had right to, but the way she figured it, any person who pulls a gun on you deserves exactly what he—or she—gets. The trigger had no idea what the sex of the person pulling it was; the bullet that could take your lights out couldn't care less.

"The granary," the sheriff said, and he lifted his chin in the direction of the neighboring building, where muzzle flashes could be seen.

There were at least two witches that Jessica could see. Both of them were holding low positions, concealing themselves behind a ventilation shaft, leaving almost no target. The space between the two buildings was less than fifteen feet, and the sheriff, fired with vengeful enthusiasm, now announced his intention.

"I'm jumping over there."

"With that hole in your shoulder?"

"It doesn't matter. I'll have time to hurt tomorrow."

One of the Welshman, a big man whose name Jessica never got, took matters into his own hands. With a sudden roar of

138

fury or determination, he took a running start and leaped toward the neighboring rooftop.

The witch's bullet caught him in mid-flight, and he hit the opposite wall with a sickening thud, fingers sliding away as he tried to maintain his grip. He fell to the alley below to lie groaning, badly wounded.

The sheriff, his determination unimpaired, shouted at Jessica Starbuck: "Cover me, lady!"

Jessica responded automatically, sending the rounds remaining in her Colt whistling toward the roof of the granary.

The sheriff, ignoring the danger to himself, hurled himself through the void between the two buildings and landed with a jarring thud on booted feet. Nevertheless he had the presence of mind to remain upright, to throw his body behind the ventilator shaft and fire back as a witch levered three rapid shots through her repeating rifle.

Bullets whined off, one narrowly missing Jessica, or so it seemed as she hit the rooftop behind the parapet and, reloading, prepared to leap across the gap between the buildings herself.

Another of the Welshmen positioned himself on the parapet and shot at the witches across the way. A bullet ripped the top of his skull away and without a sound he stepped back, turned in a slow circle and collapsed to the roof.

"Come on, if you're coming!" the sheriff yelled, and Jessica took the chance.

At that point it wasn't something she wanted to do—not after the deaths of two of their force—but the risk had to be taken. The sheriff would have no chance over there alone; besides, below Jessie the roof was getting warmer, and she could see the glow of flames through the trapdoor to the hotel roof.

She backed up, took a deep breath, and made her run.

Bullets sang all around her, the tongues of flame the burn-

139

ing black-powder grains made in the night licked at her, but she managed it. She hit the rooftop hard, rolled and dove to reach the spot the wounded sheriff had chosen as his redoubt.

Jessica didn't hear a thing, but beneath her she could feel the slightest of vibrations as someone crossed the roof toward the ventilator, and she gestured with two sharp jabs. She would take the one on the right; let the sheriff take the one creeping up from the left.

Jessie waited, her finger wrapped around the trigger of the Colt double-action revolver. Beyond the yellow-brick ventilator the flames still curled skyward, lifting smoke in a dark veil above the Colorado town. Here and there stars poked through the black screen, but they appeared dismal, small.

All of this Jessica noted only distantly. Her full attention was on the corner of the ventilator shaft, on the small vibrations of footfalls she could feel.

Still, when the witch appeared, it was with sudden savagery, unexpected despite Jessica's alertness. She carried no gun, this one. Instead her hand was wrapped around the handle of a huge bowie knife that gleamed with cold fire in the night.

Jessica rolled to one side and kicked out with both boots, sending the witch tumbling head over heels. As Jessie whirled, coming to one knee, the witch lunged at her again.

The .38 spoke twice with deadly authority, and the witch was blown backward. Simultaneously the sheriff's pistol barked, and the second witch was spun back, her face a mask of blood.

The echoes of the gunshots seemed to ring in Jessica's ears for minutes. She realized slowly that she and the lawman were simply sitting on the rooftop, that Roger Travis was standing over her, a hasty bandage around his upper arm, that Collins was still burning.

140

Roger lifted her to her feet with his good arm and then gave the wounded lawman a hand up.

"What's happening?" Jessica asked. "Rebecca?"

"She's fine," Travis assured her. "I was just worried about you. There was so much gunfire."

"The town . . . ?" the sheriff asked groggily.

"The fires are burning out. There's a lot of wounded people wandering around, a lot of dead in the streets."

"The witches?" Jessie inquired.

"Mostly gone, it seems. Those that won't be buried here. Funny the way they disappeared—like smoke from the fire," Travis said, briefly meditative. His eyes lifted to the flames and his expression was deeply thoughtful. "I never thought I'd see a day like this," he said almost under his breath.

"Manning?" Jessica Starbuck wanted to know.

"So far as I know he's gotten away cleanly. I doubt we'll ever find him. If he has any sense at all he's hightailing it for new territory after this."

"He damn well better," the sheriff, leaning against the brick ventilator, said. "I'll hang that son of a bitch for what he's done, given half the chance."

"What now?" Roger Travis asked as he, the sheriff and Jessica headed for the fire ladder that hung on the alley side of the granary.

The woman just looked at him and smiled. Those sea-green eyes were as determined as ever, her expression taut.

"Now," Jessica Starbuck replied, "I do what I came her to do. I'm pushing the Comstock Central through to Fort Vasquez, and neither weather nor Dark Masters are going to stop me. We've walked through hell, Roger, and beaten the devil. Now let's see if we can beat the timetable."

The streets below were strangely silent. Ash drifted down from out of the cold skies, and still fire fighters worked. They did see one body in a side alley, but there was really little evidence of the war that had raged through Collins in the hours before.

"I wonder," said Roger Travis, looking toward the cold, distant mountains, "about Ki. Everything seems to be under control here, but he . . ."

Too hastily Jessica said, "I know Ki. He's all right, believe me."

But he wasn't.

Chapter 17

Dan Fellows looked amiable as hell, but the rifle in his hands was as menacing as ever.

"I didn't think we'd be seeing you again," Fellows said out of the darkness. A bit ruefully, he added, "And I kinda wish I hadn't."

It was Ki's own fault and he knew it. The caverns where Manning kept his women had been dark and empty by the time he reached the river. Some searching around had produced very little, but then he had seen the dull glow of distant flames against the dark sky, and he knew something was very wrong in Fort Collins.

He pointed this out now to Fellows without much effect. "There's trouble in town, Fellows. Manning and his women, I'd guess, have been having a hell-raising night."

"So what?" Fellows said. His voice wasn't truculent, simply dispassionate. He turned his head and spat. "I really don't care what Manning's up to."

"Right or wrong?" Ki asked.

Fellows hesitated. "I don't work for Manning. I don't work for the town."

"A blind bull," Ki said mildly. He took a step toward Fellows, who had come from out of the riverside pines to halt Kiai as he tried to double back toward town. He and Archie, who always seemed to ride together, had shut down any hope of escape Ki might have had, and the *te* master had simply swung down from his horse, hands held aloft. At this last remark Fellows blinked slowly and glanced at Archie as if he had heard something in an alien language.

"A blind bull," Fellows said. "Just what in hell do you mean by that?"

"Ready to fight, not knowing what direction to charge," Ki enlarged.

"I know which way I'm going, friend—the direction the boss wants me to go."

"Even if it is the wrong direction," said Ki, glancing himself now at Archie, who looked disturbed in a vague and wistful way. "It is possible, is it not, that the 'boss' is wrong?"

"Don't matter if he's wrong," Fellows said defensively. "I ride for . . ."

"Yes," Ki interrupted harshly, "you ride for the brand. If he's right or wrong makes no difference to you."

"That's right," Fellows said, but there was something uncertain in his voice.

"Then I feel sorry for you," Kiai said, and he saw Fellows flinch with emotion. "There are few things I admire above loyalty, Fellows, but a sense of what's right and what's wrong is one of them."

"Yeah, fine," Fellows said with forced gruffness. "We'll sit and chat about it one night. All I know right now is that you're trying to talk your way out of a fix."

"I'm trying to talk you out of one," Ki replied.

"What are you talking about?"

"About the criminal activities that are going on around here, that you and you, Archie, are a part of," Ki explained. "I don't think either of you is an outlaw, but you've found a shortcut to becoming one."

Archie, his voice forced, complained, "You've got a lot

144

to talk about, Chinee. You've killed some of our people and just generally raised hell around here."

"Raised hell?" Ki kept his voice gentle. Arguing with these two men was going to do him no good, but he could sense their uneasiness with their own position. The three of them stood together in a dark and lonely pine-forest clearing. Beyond the verge of the woods, the river murmured past; and still the smoke from distant fire rose into the sky above the mountain meadows. From time to time Fellows glanced at the smoke. "I have tried to protect myself," Ki said. "I have tried to help the lady I work for keep the vultures away from what honest labor has produced."

"Wait a minute," Fellows said sharply. "What vultures are you talking about? If you mean . . ."

"Fellows," Ki answered before Dan Fellows had finished, "you know exactly what I mean. Neither of you is a stupid man. You know by now that your boss and Manning have conspired to shut down the railroad's progress so that Carl Dantley's beef can be sold to the army instead of Jessica Starbuck's cattle. You have to know that."

Dan Fellows shook his head stubbornly. A mule of a man, he was not unintelligent, as Ki had noted, but simply a creature of long habit. What he supposed or knew had nothing to do with his sense of what had to be done. Now he told Kiai exactly what that was.

"We got to take you back to the ranch, Mister."

Ki turned a frustrated face away. Even Archie groaned. "Dan," he said, "you know the man has a point. What's up here for us anyway? Why not Texas? Now, tonight!"

"Because," Dan Fellows said with heavy patience, "we hired on to do a job."

"Dan," Archie said, shaking his head, "this job ain't no good. Even I can see that."

145

"We hired on to do a job," Fellows repeated in his mulish way. "We'll do it."

"Fellows," Kiai said, spreading his hands in a gesture of supplication, "you are working for a crook. His ally is a man who has brutalized and tormented young women for his own devious purposes. As I said, believe me, I admire loyalty— I like to think that I am a loyal man—but there is a point in time when a man must see what is going on around him and not be blindly loyal. Not when the cause is an evil one."

The thought turned slowly around inside Dan Fellows's head as Archie, almost beseechingly, watched his huge partner. Finally Fellows shook his head. He seemed remorseful, but he was steadfast in his view of obligation.

"No. We're taking you back to the ranch," he said. "The boss will know what to do with you."

"The boss," Ki said bitterly, "is letting Fort Collins burn. The *boss* is letting young women be tormented and sold. The boss is taking away the livelihood of nearly a hundred good, hard-working men."

"You can just get on your horse," Dan Fellows said. "I can't listen to no more. My head's all abuzz."

"Dan . . ." Archie said, grabbing his friend by the arm, but Fellows shook him off.

"I said my head's all abuzz, Archie! I can't listen to any more talk. All I know's my job, and my job's to bring this man in."

There was no point in pursuing it further, Ki knew. He was Dantley's prisoner for the second time—and this time there would be no escape. This time there would be no pretense of a fair hearing on Carl Dantley's part. This time Ki would be taken out and executed. Maybe then Dan Fellows would realize he had made a mistake in giving all of his big heart to the "brand."

But that would do Ki no good—he would be dead.

146

They put him in the saddle of his horse and turned toward the Dantley ranch to the west. None of them spoke. The moon appeared briefly through the smoky clouds above them, and then somewhere distant thunder sounded, and the clouds began to thicken and cool. Before they reached the ranch, it had begun to rain.

In Fort Collins the citizens of the devastated town came from their homes to lift their hands thankfully toward the skies. The rain would kill what was left of the fires that had been burning through the night; and in the morning, if there was reconstruction to be done, at least there would be a foundation left to build upon.

Rebecca had returned from the train. Her defiant, world-challenging glare had gone, and in the dying light of the flames Jessie saw a different woman. A child, nearly. She stared at the destruction around her as if she had never dreamed such things could happen. But Jessica knew it wasn't the fire, the rain, Rebecca was thinking of.

"Ki . . . where is he?" Manning's daughter asked softly.

"He's all right," Jessica said without really believing it herself. "He'll be back soon."

"I know him well enough to know that he would have been here—where there was trouble—if he could have," Rebecca Manning said.

Jessica knew that as well, but he would have ridden a long distance by the time the flames started to color the sky—perhaps he hadn't been able to make it in time. Still she wondered, as did Rebecca. Jessica repeated it, as if saying it often enough would make it so: "He's all right."

"What do we do now?" Travis asked.

"Just what I told you," Jessica answered. "What I came here to do." She squeezed his hand once. The doctor emerged from his operating room with a pale sheriff trailing after him, arm in a sling, eyes more angry than pained.

"Sorry, lady," the lawman said and Jessica believed he really was. "I should've listened to you all. I just didn't think those people were crazy enough to attack my town—and my town comes first."

"All right," Jessica said evenly. "Let's get past that now. We've got work to do. But, tell me this, Sheriff, what do you think was going to happen to your town once the railroad pulled out, once the wages of our people were yanked out of your economy?" The sheriff frowned in puzzlement. Jessica let the matter drop. "What we have to do now is get to work. Roger, can you find Bob Sachs? Sheriff, I want to have a meeting not only with the timbermen and the track-layers, but with the people of this town. It's time we all got together and defeated these people who set fire to Collins."

"Defeat them, how?" the sheriff asked. "You mean go up there and look for this Manning and his women?"

"No. There's a simpler way. What will he have to fight for once the line is pushed through to Fort Vasquez? The way to defeat them is to get the job done."

"Jessica," Travis said, "it may not work, but I'd like to try wiring Vasquez again to see if we can get some troops to help you lay iron."

"Try it. It can't hurt. Meanwhile," she went on, "I want to talk to my own people again. They're angry now—and they've seen that these witches aren't supernatural. They can be put down with lead. I'm sorry as hell for these women, truly, but this railroad is going through one way or the other, and if Manning chooses to send more of them to their death, I can't do anything to stop it.

"The railroad," she repeated strongly, "is going through."

By the time Bob Sachs showed up, the meeting hall was

full of impatient and still-angry men. Not only were the Welsh and Chinese timbermen and tracklayers there in full force, but the townspeople were well represented. They listened to Jessica, who made a short and forceful speech, and by the time the dawn was breaking, there were few who weren't in agreement with the main points she made.

"The town needs the railroad. You working men need your wages. The army needs the beef. Once the line is driven through to Vasquez, these troublemakers in the mountains will be gone. Let's do it together!"

A low murmur of agreement turned into a roar of assent as the men present, angry and determined to do something to solve the situation, rose to their feet in the town hall. The only negative point of the evening was a ragged-looking Roger Travis, who had to return with the news: "The army can't or won't help. The colonel considers it strictly a civilian matter. He's still ready to buy cattle from Dantley. Sorry, Jessica, it's hard to put the facts in a telegram. He doesn't understand what we've been dealing with down here. He only wants to feed his troopers."

It was difficult to blame the commanding officer at Vasquez for that. Jessica was never one for worrying about problems she couldn't solve. Now she turned her attention to Bob Sachs and the men gathered around her. She turned her attention to the solution, not the problem: "All right—this is what has to be done. We're going to lay track to Vasquez faster than Carl Dantley can drive a herd there."

"It can't be done!" a tracklayer exclaimed.

"Maybe not, but we're sure as hell going to try, mister. We've got the men and we've got the motivation. Let's give it our best. Let's beat these crooks!"

Chapter 18

The sunlight was in Rebecca Manning's eyes when she awoke. It streamed through the pale blue curtains of her room and struck her in the eyes. How and when she had fallen asleep, she did not know.

She had awakened too suddenly from a dream in which Kiai held her tightly in his strong arms and spoke soft, unintelligible words into her ears as his hands stroked her body.

Now she realized that there was turmoil outside her window, and she bounded from her bed too quickly, to cross, nude, to the window. In the streets men were moving in all directions.

Horses and wagons loaded with green lumber streamed toward the railroad tracks; and from there a whistle blew shrilly, a bell clanged and steam escaped into the bright, pale blue morning skies.

In the middle of the human maelstrom, Rebecca saw Jessica Starbuck, mounted now on a little dun horse, shouting instructions through cupped hands. Rebecca, with a heavy sigh, went back to her bed and sat there for long minutes before she sagged back to stare at the ceiling and then slowly close her eyes and try to recapture her dream.

Jessica couldn't afford the luxury of dreaming.

From the warehouse near Jules Jenkins's depot, steel rails were being loaded onto flat cars. The train, inching forward along gleaming new track, hauled these as the teamsters passing Jessica on either side hauled ties and bridge timbers. At Game Trail Camp Bob Sachs had his crews, augmented by some local volunteers, cutting timber, sawing to length, planing it, and the ties were coming down from the hills in a steady procession.

Riding north of the town, Jessica watched as the work went on at a furious pace. The railroad bed had been graded long ago, and outside of redistributing crushed rock here and there, it was ready to be worked, and work it they did.

From the wagons, timbers were yanked and tossed to waiting men who picked them up and laid them on the bed. From the train creeping along behind them, Chinese carried the rails, three men to a rail, and brawny Welshmen with sledges and spikes pinned them in place.

"Damn all," Roger Travis said, walking up to Jessica, "if I don't think you just might be able to do it at this rate."

"How're things over the mountains?" Jessica asked.

"The herd's still bedded down. There's no sign yet that Dantley knows he's in a race."

"Ki?" she asked hopefully.

"I didn't see him. I tried following his tracks for a while, but lost him before the river. He may have headed for the caves, may have not. I steered clear of them myself."

"That was best," Jessica admitted. Ki hadn't been heading that way without an exact idea of what he was up to. Jessica didn't know his plan in detail; but she knew that Roger Travis, despite his courage and abilities, wasn't going to be able to help Ki, only to get himself in trouble as well.

But where are you, Ki?

"He'll be all right," Roger Travis said, seeming to read her thoughts. "But, Jessica, you can't believe they'll just give up—Manning and Dantley, I mean. They can't afford

151

to let you beat them, with the investment they have in this, can they?"

"No, they can't afford it. There'll be trouble still, Roger. A lot of trouble."

"Is there anything we can do in the meantime?"

"Stay armed," the lady said, "stay alert—and lay steel like hell."

All of that would do no good. The railroad construction didn't go unnoticed.

Manning, his eyes wilder than ever, arrived at Carl Dantley's ranch sometime after noon. He swung down from his horse, and with his cape swirling, stormed toward the door of the log house where Dantley with expressionless eyes waited.

"Well?" Manning demanded impatiently.

"Well, what?" Carl Dantley asked. He had no idea what the man was on about this time, and the truth was he was tired of Manning altogether and half-regretted the day he had got into this crazy scheme.

Except there was still big money to be had out of it.

"What?" Manning said in exasperation, pushing past Dantley to enter the house. "The railroad—that's what!"

"I don't know what you mean," the Texas cattleman said quietly. Where he had been brought up, even adversaries observed the common civilities. You didn't just walk into a man's house uninvited, and you didn't act as if you owned it once you were inside.

"Of course you wouldn't know," Manning, obviously agitated, answered. He waved a hand in the air. "They're driving through to Fort Vasquez."

"They're what?" This was a different matter. The cattle Dantley was holding on his range were damn near his total financial resources. If this madman was telling the truth, he

152

was about to lose everything he had in the world. "Who told you that?"

"Nobody told me, damn you!" Manning answered furiously. "I saw them. They're laying track up the line."

"Without ties?"

"Not without ties," Manning said in a way abrasive enough for Dantley to lift his eyebrows in annoyance. "Somehow they've gotten the timbermen to go back to work."

Dantley stood stock-still for a minute and then began to pace his floor methodically, his mind slowly revolving.

"How many people have they got working? Half of them? A quarter?"

"All of them as near as I can tell," Manning answered with a perverse smugness. "Plus half the townspeople."

"What in hell could have caused . . . What have you been up to, Manning?"

"What do you mean?" Manning said evasively. He knew well enough what Dantley meant. The raid on the town had galvanized it to action. He was damned if he was going to admit it, however, or take responsibility for what seemed to be the crumbling of their grand scheme.

"Never mind," Dantley said, resuming his pacing. "What has to be done now is to solve things. We can't let them beat us to Vasquez—if we do, all of this has been for nothing."

"All right, then," Manning snarled. "We'll stop them. We'll attack and attack!"

"Doesn't seem smart to me," Dantley said, and the warlock gave him a scathing glance.

"You just said that they had to be stopped. What are you going to do? Start your herd toward Fort Vasquez and hope to beat the railroad there?"

"That and something else I've had in mind, yeah," Dantley answered. The rancher was at the window now, looking

153

out at his herd, the slowly circling cowboys and the timbered hills around him.

"What?" Manning was impatient. He wanted to strike back and hard. He hadn't managed to get Rebecca back, had lost numbers of his women in the fight in town, and now it appeared the entire grand scheme was crumbling. How Dantley could take it calmly was beyond the warlock.

"Maybe a trade-off," Dantley said, turning from the window. His stubby brown fingers scratched the stubble on his throat. "Maybe I've got something the woman wants more than she wants the train to get through to Vasquez."

"I don't know what you're talking about," Manning said angrily. "All I want you to do is mount your men and give them their rifles. Those townspeople aren't going to stand up in a gunfight, not for the sake of the Starbuck Empire." The speech was wasted on the cattle baron, who seemed to be paying no attention to Manning's raving.

"Come with me," Dantley said finally. He crooked a finger and opened a heavy door that led onto a long dark hallway.

"What is this?" Manning asked mistrustfully.

Dantley just inclined his head and started down the corridor. At the end of it, Manning could see a cowboy tilted back in a wooden chair, hat pulled low, rifle across his lap. There was a pile of clothes—black jeans, a leather vest, cork-soled slippers—near the door at the end of the corridor.

Manning was apprehensive. "What are you up to here, Dantley?" he asked.

The cattleman laughed. "What's the matter, Manning? Afraid I'm going to lock you up or something? I don't go back on my partners. You've done your best to help us out. Now I'm going to show you the ace in the hole that's going to pull us out of this without any more shooting. Take a look,'' Carl Dantley said, indicating the small barred window set into the door.

Manning approached the window hesitantly, but once he peered inside he began to smile and then to laugh until he had to cling to the bars of the window to keep from falling. His body trembled convulsively and his peals of laughter echoed up the corridor, until Archie, who was the man sitting guard there, turned his head away in disgust. *Mad*, Archie thought silently, violently. And he wasn't far from wrong.

There might have been something humorous about a naked man in manacles locked up in a cold storage room, but whatever that might have been, it eluded Archie, who was made of simpler stuff.

''You've got him!'' Manning said triumphantly as if they had just won a war. Then he turned toward Dantley and clapped him on the shoulder, a gesture which made the cattleman flinch. ''Damn it all, you've got the son of a bitch!''

Manning turned back toward the window of Ki's cell with undisguised glee. ''Chains! Where'd you come by those, Dantley?'' the leader of the witches asked. Dantley muttered an answer. To him it seemed that Manning was enjoying the prisoner's humiliation more than the ramifications that Ki's recapture had for saving their plans.

''Always kept 'em around. Now and then we used to have a hand go crazy drunk and start waving guns around. They're useful.''

''But this is wonderful!'' Manning said, as if the implications had only just come home.

''It'll work'' was Dantley's terse response.

''Of course.'' Manning now began to pace in short, measured steps. ''We'll ask Starbuck if she wants him back. The trade is the railroad for the man's life. If she shuts down the construction, the Chinaman lives, if she refuses, well—he'll pay the price.''

155

"Yeah," Carl Dantley said. Again, it seemed that Manning was more excited by the possibility of Ki's death than in the workings of the plan. The rancher glanced at his hired hand, but Archie was studiously observing the floor. Obviously the cowhand liked none of this. Dantley was beginning to have his own doubts, but damn all, *something* had to be done. There was too much at stake—time, money, cattle.

He had been aware for some time that most of his men, even the staunchest, like Dan Fellows, had no taste for what was going on, that working with the likes of the deranged Manning went against their grain. Well, that was too damn bad! It had to be this way or they all would go under.

Manning had returned to the cell window to grip the bars tightly, his forehead against the cool iron.

"Where's my daughter?" he asked Ki in a hissing voice.

Slowly the *te* master's head came up. He answered with quiet dignity. "Safe, one would hope. Away from the terror you have made her life."

"Bastard!" Manning growled. Ki would not be baited. He continued to sit naked, cross-legged on the floor in a semi-lotus position, his manacled hands folded across his lap.

He knew what was afoot, of course, and he knew that Jessica would give in if it was a matter of his life against the life of the Comstock Central. She did not need the railroad to survive; there was almost too much money at her disposal. For the sake of her friend, Jessica would do almost anything—and to abandon the railroad just when she was on the verge of defeating these two hoodlums would be simple if it meant Ki's well-being.

Ki was not sure it would mean anything of the kind.

Carl Dantley, for all of his underhanded ways, was basically a man of honor, it seemed to Ki. He was a man used to running things his way, bulling ahead, fighting if it took

156

that, confident always in his own rightness and right to rule. But if he told Jessica that they had a bargain, Ki thought he was the kind to stick to it even if it galled him.

Manning was a different story.

If Archie and even Dantley had the suspicion that the warlock was mad, Kiai had no doubts at all. He had seen too much of his work; he knew Rebecca too well.

If Dantley planned on doing what to his code was honorable—that is, winning the fight with Jessica Starbuck, but keeping his word to turn Ki over when it was done, Manning couldn't be trusted to live up to even that primitive sort of ethics.

If he had the chance, he would kill Ki.

That left the samurai with no choice. He would have to escape and make his own way back to Fort Collins. The manacles were no problem. Long ago, in a monastery in Japan, Ki had learned the art of dislocating his thumbs to slip his hands from such bonds. But slipping the manacles would do him no appreciable good. They had taken his clothes; they had posted an armed guard. He could hardly flee naked and unarmed across the mountains. The man who watched him now was much better than the guard who had watched him the first time. And, the ceiling to the storeroom had been rebuilt, the planks fastened down with bolts.

It seemed that they had lost. Jessica would lose the beef contract and the railroad. Manning and Dantley would become wealthy men. It was total defeat. What else could go wrong?

"I want my daughter back, too," Manning said outside Ki's cell window, and Ki flinched with anger.

"You want what?" Dantley asked.

"When we make the bargain with the Starbuck woman," Manning said, "we'll promise her the life of the Chinaman; but I want to make sure I get Rebecca back as well." The

157

warlock paused for a long minute as his chest rose and fell with emotion. "Rebecca must come back to me, Dantley. She will have to learn a lesson. A very hard lesson. No one of my people can leave me. And you see what it would mean to the others if my own daughter can leave the coven, don't you? She must be a part of the bargain, Dantley. Don't forget it!"

The last few words were spat out with such virulence that even Dantley felt a cold finger of fear touch his spine. But it was Ki who felt anger, a mad passion that only his Eastern training could cool and slowly calm as he meditated on more peaceful thoughts. The anger faded eventually, but not the knowledge.

He would, he knew, have to kill Manning.

Chapter 19

"The herd's up," Roger Travis reported to Jessie. He had come to the railhead to meet her. Bob Sachs had just departed, complaining about the logistics of moving the rail ties as the train crept farther from Game Trail Camp. Two wagons had broken axles moving across the rough ground beside the rail line, and a belt on one of the huge timber-camp buzzsaws had snapped.

Jessica, railroad map in her hand, turned toward Travis, who had just swung down from his army bay horse. Already, she knew, he was close to being overdue at Fort Vasquez, but he had stayed on to the last possible minute to try to help Jessie.

"He knows, then?" she asked.

"He must. They've got the herd up and they're being pushed this way—fast." Travis removed his hat, wiped his forehead and took a swing from the canteen hanging from the cantle of his saddle. His voice was slightly puzzled as he added, "But not as fast as you'd expect."

"What do you mean?" Beyond the spot where they spoke, the hammers rang constantly as track was layed, there was continuous shouting as the men worked and more than an occasional curse. The locomotive exhaled steam from its relief valves as it crawled forward, up the grade which wound through the deep blue-spruce woods.

"If I were Dantley," Travis explained, "I'd be damn near running that herd. Or," he said alternately, "I'd be trying my best to shut the railroad down. He knows that if you get through to Vasquez, you've proved up on the contract, and that if you don't, the colonel's sure as hell going to be looking for beef the first place he can turn. The herd's up and moving, but it's almost a businesslike pace. It's almost like Dantley figures he's got cards up his sleeve and already figures he's won."

"What could he have?" Jessica wondered aloud. If Dantley and Manning knew her reputation at all, they would know she wouldn't quit until the last dog had died. She would push the Comstock through to Vasquez if she had to throw her shoulder behind the caboose and push it there with main strength.

It didn't figure. Ki didn't enter her thoughts.

She turned and bawled out to the workers passing by, "Let's lay some steel, men! They're not going to beat us now."

Dantley had other thoughts.

He figured he had won the game, and by his rules, he had won the game squarely. Let the little lady lay all the steel she wanted. There was no way she was going to beat him to Vasquez, and there was no way she was going to even try after she found out that he had the Chinaman hostage.

It was a strange sort of cattle drive. Carl Dantley had driven herds up the Santa Fe Trail and over the Bozeman, but this was a job that bordered on unreality.

Dan Fellows was thinking much the same thing. He was riding swing, but in reality he was only a guard for the prisoner. He slouched in his Denver saddle and squinted into the sunlight, watching the silent, erect Kiai, still wearing manacles, mounted on a blood-red bay that was well known

160

among the hands as the slowest, most decrepit, useless horse in the remuda. Carl Dantley was not going to take the chance of mounting the Chinese on a decent pony.

Not that Kiai would have been able to escape if he were riding the quickest little darter the brand had to offer. Manacled, with armed men surrounding him, with Dan Fellows's always-vigilant eyes on him, he was going nowhere.

Fellows shifted his eyes briefly, noting the cowboys working the mixed Hereford-longhorn herd, the dust streaming into the pale sky, and the odd contingent accompanying them.

For beside the herd, riding tightly bunched, was a party of perhaps twenty women in black dresses, and at their head, the bull of the herd, the warlock Manning.

Fellows had no taste for riding herd on a manacled prisoner—he would rather have been doing his job, managing the cattle—and he had no taste for Manning and his band of witches, but the Texan clamped his jaw shut and rode on, the rifle across the saddlebows constantly pointed in Kiai's direction.

Ki held the ancient bay to its course with knee pressure. The horse was old, but it had been well trained in its time and responded as any good buffalo horse or cowpony did to the touch of a knee. That did Ki no good either. The truth was, if he had had his *shuriken* or a gun it would have done him no good. There was simply no escape.

Fellows was watching him hawklike, but it was Manning who worried Ki—an almost maniacal glare was fixed on Kiai each time he glanced in the direction of the warlock.

From time to time murmured conversation or instructions passed between Manning and his witches. Ki didn't need to hear the words to understand what they were talking about. The pale-faced women stared at him with vacant animosity as if Ki threatened their leader, their cult, the Dark Master himself.

161

He had no doubt that Dan Fellows, trying to do the job he had been given, would cut him down if he tried to make a run for it.

He had no doubt that Manning and the witches were going to kill him no matter what. Kill all they could when they could in some sort of orgiastic offering to their Dark Master. Ki said to Fellows, "The man's insane."

It was a long time before Dan Fellows answered. When he did it was only two words, "Is he?"

"You know he is. Why are you tied up with people like these, Fellows?"

"I'm not tied up with them," Fellows said, still speaking grudgingly as if each word were a betrayal of his employer and his obligation.

"It looks like you're riding the same trail," Ki observed.

"Yeah, and so are you, but I'm not tied up with you," Fellows growled.

"But why . . . ?" Ki began, but Dan Fellows cut him off with uncharacteristic heat.

"Listen, I'm doing a job, okay! It'll be done soon and I'll be out of here, me and Archie back toward Texas. For now I'm doing the damn job."

"No matter what."

"No matter what," Fellows answered. He swore under his breath and then asked, "Why don't you just ride silent, partner? You'll be out of this soon enough."

"Will I?"

"The boss says so. I take him at his word."

"And Manning?"

"I got nothing to do with him."

"You've got a lot to do with him," Ki corrected. "And when he's arrested for murder and arson and torture, you may be required to explain why you sat your saddle and did nothing. When the government wants to know who sabotaged

162

their beef supplier's railroad, you may be asked why you sat your saddle. You may, in fact, find yourself behind bars for a good many years, Fellows.''

"Shut up, just shut up!'' Dan Fellows said, and his face said it all—he knew damn well that all of this was wrong. He was just a man who had hired on to do a job, and the job had gotten very dirty.

They started the herd up over a wooded knoll now, and Ki became more alert although he pretended to be more accepting of his fate, to drowse in the saddle and be docilely herded along, one more steer pushed wherever the cattlemen wished to push him.

He was far from that docile.

Ki knew that whatever Dantley or Fellows had decided to do with him, Manning had already made up his mind that he would die.

He could die trying to escape or die where they chose to kill him. The choice wasn't much no matter how you looked at it, but he had already determined to make his try for it, and as they entered the timber, it seemed he had his chance.

Fellows was still alert, but even he had his failures. As the cattle labored up the slope, one of them was accidentally gored. A calf bawled, a steer bolted and soon the entire herd moved nervously in many directions. Fellows's head swung toward the scene, and Ki heeled the old bay he was riding—hard.

The horse took two leaping steps toward the timber and then with Ki's continued encouragement lined out through the woods, neck stretched out, tail pluming with motion. Ki heard a rifle shot and ducked low.

It had to have been Fellows who fired, and Ki thought, it had to be that he hadn't taken his best shot, for the slug flew far wide of its mark, thudding into the trunk of a big woodpecker-pocked pine.

As he rode, the samurai slipped the manacles from his wrists. Behind him he could hear the sounds of pursuit as Dantley's cowboys and Manning's crazed witches took up the trail. There was much cursing and wild shrieking and one ill-advised shot aimed at a target Ki could only guess at.

The panicked bay horse went halfway to its haunches as it slid down the pine needle–covered slope above the rill and Ki cast his manacles aside.

Above and behind him he could still hear shouts and curses, but it was obvious that—for the time being—they had lost his trail.

Ki wound upslope through the timber, hearing again a distant shot that must have been aimed at a ghost of someone's imagination. He crested the ridge and almost laughed with surprise and relief. He saw below him, above the tips of the pines, smoke rising from the diamond stack of a locomotive, and as weary as the horse might have been, he tagged it hard with his heels and lifted it into a hard downhill run, toward the railroad line and safety.

If Dantley was unhappy, Manning was furious. The warlock sat his horse, staring down at the railroad's progress, knowing he had lost Kiai, Rebecca, and probably the race toward Vasquez in one fell swoop.

"Now we have to do it my way," Manning shouted wildly at the cattleman. Dantley looked with genuine distaste at his partner in crime, wondering how he had ever let himself get hooked into this in the first place.

The two men had dismounted and stood together in a clearing on a timbered slope. Behind Manning like a flock of crows stood his witches, silent, obedient as they held their horses. On the ridge above them the herd continued to move northward through the trees as a few searchers below the two looked with waning hope for Kiai.

"Your way's mad," Carl Dantley said, shifting his rifle from one hand to the other.

Manning stiffened. "I don't like that word; don't use that word," the warlock answered.

"I'm just trying to say it won't work," Dantley substituted. "They got the numbers on us, Manning."

"You've got plenty of men. We can strike without warning, snipe at them from out of the trees. When the Chinese and the Welsh see my witches, they'll take to their heels anyway. The sheriff you know," Manning added with a sneer. "He'll not fight."

"Things have changed, Manning. I'm not so sure about any of that."

"Look," Manning said, and he turned to point upslope where the cattle plodded on patiently. "What are you going to do with your herd? Eat them all? Turn back toward home? It'll snow soon and there won't be any trail graze. I'll wager you can't pay your men now. Can you? You think they're going to drive the herd back south without pay?"

Dantley shook his head worriedly. All of these thoughts had been going through his own head, but as he had said, everything had changed. Letting Manning frighten off the workers and delay the railroad until the army had no choice but to buy his herd had seemed like a smart idea, and a safe enough one for Dantley, who only had to hold the herd and then when the time came push them through to Fort Vasquez.

Now he was caught up in something entirely different. Manning proposed making war on the railroad workers and half the town. He stared at the ground and then lifted his eyes again to the ridge, where the men riding drag were pushing the last of the herd out of vision.

"That's your life up there, isn't it?" Manning nudged. "All the investment of a life's labor. I thought you had guts,"

165

the warlock sniffed. "Fight for what you want. We've come too far to back down now."

Dantley still shook his head stubbornly, but Manning was right about it all. He would lose the herd if he couldn't pay his hands. And if he lost the herd, he would lose the home ranch and everything else he had.

A lifetime's work down the drain.

Disgusted with himself and with Manning, the cattleman spun away and swung into the saddle. He sat there for a long minute staring down at the warlock.

"All right, then, damn it! We'll try it your way."

Manning could have his war.

Chapter 20

Roger Travis whistled shrilly, and when Jessica's head came up from her surveying map, she let out a little cry of relief. Travis was pointing across the dell where the laying of the railroad bed continued. There, riding up through a thicket of red fern and blackjack was a tall man on a bay horse.

"Ki!" she said with whispered emotion, and then, with the army lieutenant's arm around her, she stood waiting for Kiai to arrive.

He looked well enough except for a bruise on his forehead. He walked his horse across the newly laid track and swung down, grinning as Jessica walked to him and embraced him.

"You show up when you feel like it, don't you?" she asked teasingly.

"When I am allowed," Ki answered.

It took awhile, but Ki told the story of his recapture while Jessica and Travis listened intently. Ki had noticed immediately that Travis was in uniform now, gauntlets on, his horse equipped with saddlebags. At the conclusion of his story he mentioned it.

"You are leaving."

"There's no choice, Ki. Orders. I tried to stick as long as possible, but I'm right to the deadline now."

Ki glanced at Jessica, who seemed unhappy thinking about

167

the lieutenant's departure, but all of them knew he could not ignore orders.

"What will you report?" Ki asked.

"The truth as I best know it," Travis answered with a shrug. "The trouble is that even when the line has reached Vasquez, the Comstock will still have to make a return run. I don't know how long the colonel can wait for provisions."

"But in the long run . . ."

"Of course, in the long run everyone at Vasquez—and at Fort Collins—will be better off, but the colonel has his duty as well. I can't fault him for thinking of his troopers first."

"How are we doing on time, Jessica?" Ki asked.

"Two days with any luck. The skies are clear and we've got plenty of help."

"And for Dantley to push his herd through? What would you guess, approximately the same?"

"I would think so," Jessica answered. It would be nip and tuck.

Ki's mouth tightened a little, but he said nothing. It could be this grand effort was coming too late. Unless Travis could convince the colonel to give them a brief extension, they had lost to Dantley and Manning.

Travis now pulled his watch from his pocket, glanced at it unhappily and shook his head. "I've got to be going, Jessie. You know how little I want to, but it has to be done."

"I know."

"I'll talk to the colonel. I'll try to make him understand, I promise."

"Thanks. That's all we can ask for. An extra day or so beyond the deadline."

Travis squeezed her shoulder briefly and then spun away to swing up into the saddle. Jessica followed him. Resting her hand on his thigh, she looked up at the mounted cavalry officer.

168

"Do you want me to ride a little way with you?" she asked and Travis grinned.

"Yeah," he replied, "just a little way."

The surveyor's map was passed to Ki, who rolled it more tightly in his hands, and Jessica walked to where her picketed pony grazed. She swung aboard and rode back to Travis and Ki.

"You can watch things, can't you, Ki?"

"For as long as necessary," Ki answered with a trace of a smile. "Ride as far as you wish."

Travis didn't wish to ride far, nor did Jessica Starbuck. They rode only far enough to leave the sounds of hammering and those of the clanking locomotive behind, to lose the scent of the wood-burning train, the shouts of the men, the cursing in three languages.

They swung down from their horses in a pine-and-cedar-screened teacup valley no more than half an acre across. There the cold wind, its edge blunted by the trees, did not touch them, and on that side of the hill the sun shone warmly.

Jessica Starbuck slipped from her horse's back and stood waiting for her man.

Roger Travis walked to her, leaving his hat hung on the pommel of his saddle. Smiling, he took her into his arms and held her closely for a long minute. Then he stepped back a little, and his fingers trailed down across her breasts. He kissed Jessica again, lightly, and began slowly to unbutton her shirt, letting his lips follow the trail his fingers made as her hands rested behind his neck, encouraging him.

His lips went to her nipples as her breasts sprang free, and he gently, slowly suckled there, his teeth once nipping at the pink, tender flesh.

Jessica laughed, untucked her shirt and threw it aside. She unbuckled her pants and sat on her shirt to tug them and her

169

boots off. She lay gloriously naked in the warm sunlight, butterflies hovering above the long meadow grass.

Travis, naked himself now, went down to her, letting his mouth follow the contours of her body—thighs, abdomen, sleek neck, ears and forehead.

"Over," Jessica said, for she was beginning to warm, to loosen, her body to become damp and sweeter for him. Travis, his fingers tangled in her honey-blond hair obliged, rolling onto his back, his forearm thrown over his eyes as Jessica returned the touches he had been giving her.

Her hands ran across his hard-muscled thighs to his groin, where his rigid manhood pulsed beneath her grip. She kissed him lightly and smiled up at him, her eyes alight with desire.

Slowly, too slowly, for Travis, she lifted herself and straddled his body, gazing down into his eyes as she positioned him and slowly sank onto his shaft, taking it to its limit.

Travis's eyes were closed. His hands were busy stroking her smooth, firm ass, running across her breasts, touching her warm dampness, the now erect tab of flesh that lay hidden behind the soft down at the juncture of her thighs.

Jessica responded heatedly. Her body, which had been gently rising and falling, now began to increase its motion, to rock and sway against his pelvis as he gripped her ass tightly with both hands.

She could no longer control the pulsing of her body, its surging need, any more than she could control the wind sweeping across the mountain meadow, and she slammed against him, biting hard at her lower lip, her eyes closed in deep physical concentration as Travis, beneath her, bucked against Jessie, searching for his own climax.

She suddenly dipped her head and searched his face with her lips, kissing his mouth, neck, shoulders and chest as the rising spasms in her body built to a crest and warm fluid drained from her body.

Travis could hold back no more. He arched his back hard and repeatedly until Jessie felt as if she were riding a bucking stallion. He began to tremble beneath her, and with one final, wrenching thrust, he came deeply, dragging her mouth to his for a long, tooth-grating, lip-punishing kiss.

They lay there silently, arms wrapped around each other, catching their breath as the warm sun touched their already heated bodies and the cool wind whispered past.

Then the shooting began near the rail line and they leaped to their feet, grabbing for their clothes. Somehow Jessica already knew what was happening.

The witches were coming again.

Ki had been observing the work on the line, following the surveyor's stakes ahead of the laborers, from time to time helping to line track or spell a man. His thoughts strayed to Rebecca occasionally, but she was safe in Fort Collins, and for now, this was more important.

The sheriff and his deputy had ridden up the line, the sheriff's arm now in a sling. He was obviously uncomfortable but hadn't appeared to be in much pain.

"Laudanum," the sheriff growled when Ki had asked him. "Could hardly stay on my horse. Damn near rather have the pain than doze when I have work to do."

It seemed to Ki that the sheriff spent most of his time dozing when he had work to do anyway, but he didn't say anything so impolitic.

The deputy, long-eared, narrow-faced, was swinging down to join them when Ki asked, "And how has it been for you?"

The man never answered. A bullet ripped through his chest, puffing out the back of his vest in a ragged explosion. He seemed to nod to Ki and then fall across the tracks, dead.

That was the first shot.

By the time Jessica and Travis, riding at a dead run, reached the tracks again, there were three more men down,

171

one of them writhing in agony. From behind trees and from inside the train, men exchanged shots with witches and Dantley's hired guns.

Jessica had her mount shot out from under her. She felt the thud of the bullet hitting the pony's neck, felt it falter and then begin to lose its knees.

She kicked out of the stirrups and leaped for safety just as the horse began a head-over roll. She landed with stunning force and crawled for a little way before she came to her feet to stand wobbly and confused, bullets singing past her.

Roger Travis was there suddenly. Slowing his horse, he gripped Jessie's wrist and swung her up behind him as he quirted the bay toward the train and shelter.

The foaming army horse was drawn up sharply and both Jessie and Travis dismounted before the shuddering animal had come to a complete stop.

Bullets were aimed at the train on this side, too, and Travis, more out of anger than a hope of hitting anything, sent three shots through the barrel of his Schofield revolver in the direction of the snipers.

Jessica had already leaped aboard the train, and Travis was behind her now, taking three running steps to hit the platform between the two Pullman cars. He ducked inside just as a slug from somewhere ricocheted off the door frame beside his head, sending hot, fragmented lead spinning off into the day.

Jessica had tripped going through the door, her head still confused from the fall, but a strong, familiar hand yanked her to her feet as Travis rushed into the Pullman.

"You are all right?" Ki asked, and she managed a half-smile and a nod.

"Yeah."

For a moment Ki thought she was going to collapse into one of the plush red seats of the car, but Jessica Starbuck was made of finer stuff than that. Her frontier stock rose to the surface and her father's blood grew hotter. She unholstered her slate-gray .38 with its peachwood grips and moved to a window, keeping her head low, and one of Dantley's overeager gunhands paid a price as he burst from the trees, spurring his horse toward the train.

Jessica's pistol spoke twice, and horse and rider went tumbling to the ground, the horse rising to shake its head and trot away, reins trailing.

The gunhand stayed where he was, a bullet through his heart.

Ki had his own problems on the opposite side of the Pullman.

Six mounted men had burst from the woods, and now their bullets crackled through the air, ringing off the side of the railroad car, shattering the plate glass windows of the Pullman.

Ki rose up and, with his rifle butt, smashed out the remaining glass in the frame he crouched behind, levering through three shots at the hard-riding, approaching gunmen. One of them tagged flesh, and he saw the man fall to the ground and be dragged along by his horse as his boot stuck in stirrup leather.

Then again Ki was forced to duck, driven to the floor by a hailstorm of bullets. Through the window something even deadlier flew over his head. A jacket dowsed with kerosene, ignited on the run by the gunmen, sailed past Ki, and within seconds the Pullman was afire while outside the guns boomed challengingly.

Ki leaped to his feet but tripped over an iron seat bracket. He went down hard and rolled onto his back in time to see the mounted gunman through the broken window stand in his stirrups and aim the Winchester in his direction.

173

★

Chapter 21

Flames had begun to sheet up the wall of the Pullman even before Ki hit the floor. His rifle had clattered away out of his grip. Now the face of Dantley's hired gun loomed in the window above him, and Ki had time to notice the sneer on the cowboy's face before it was wiped away in a fog of blood.

A bullet ripped into the oak flooring beside Ki's arm, but it was a badly aimed shot. Dead men don't shoot well.

Jessica Starbuck's .38 bullet had hit the gunfighter squarely in the face, driving up through cheekbone and brain to exit nastily through the top of his skull, and he toppled back from the saddle.

Ki managed to wink at Jessica in appreciation. He was a man of courage, but his body trembled slightly as he tried to rise. He knew how close he had come to meeting his own Dark Master, if such a thing there was.

It had saved his life, that snap shot she had gotten off, but it hadn't done a thing to put out the fire, which was now raging through the Pullman. Ki ducked low, grabbed Jessica by the hand, and with Travis behind them, they fought their way through the smoke toward the door, knowing that outside bullets and more hellfire waited for them.

One of the railroad crew lay dead on the steps of the Pullman car. A cowboy lay dying against the grass beside the tracks. Manning was poisoning the world with his madness, it seemed.

Smoke from the burning passenger car billowed into the skies, and Jessica shouted at Ki.

"Yank the pin! I won't lose the whole train."

Then she was gone, leaving it to Ki to drop the chains and the coupling pin holding the Pullman to the forward part of the train.

Jessica, moving in a crouch, ran toward the locomotive, which still had a head of steam up. The engineer, rifle in his hands, was lying flat on the rolled steel floor of his cab. His eyes came up in fear as Jessica launched herself toward him, but settled to concern.

Jessica glanced up the tracks, seeing enough laid steel to do what they needed to do.

"Move us up the tracks," she commanded. "We've got a fire in the car behind us!"

"Miss Starbuck . . ." The engineer was obviously afraid to rise while the bullets still flew, pinging off the boiler of the locomotive.

"Do it, or I'll do it!" she shouted back.

The man rose to his feet, a hunched figure moving toward the controls. He yanked two levers back, and the train lurched forward, nearly sending Jessica to the floor.

She held on and kept fighting.

Most of her men had been armed, but they had been caught unaware and now lay with hands over their heads on the grass or were fleeing to the forest. It wasn't the sight of Manning's witches that frightened them, but the banging of the gunfighters' guns.

Jessie, on one knee, two-handed her pistol and popped away at the incoming riders who flanked the train like Indians riding past at top speed. She saw Travis and Ki running to catch up with her and then, from the corner of her eye, yet another gunman. Her sights switched to the man in the duster and whoever he was—or had been—he went down with a bullet through lungs and heart.

Ki hit the locomotive steps and rolled into the cab. Seconds later Travis was there, clinging to the handrail of the steps as he fired back at a party of advancing gunhands.

He took one from the saddle and sent a second back to the woods with a wounded shoulder before his service revolver's hammer snapped down on an empty cylinder and he, too, took shelter in the cab of the iron-gray locomotive.

Behind them Jessica could see the flaming Pullman fall away as they moved up the tracks, but there was no chance of riding the locomotive to safety. They had plain run out of track.

And from the west the witches attacked.

The engineer went down as a bullet ripped through his body from side to side, breaking ribs, and Ki had to leap to the controls to stall out the locomotive, which would have kept running on a naked railbed.

The shrill of braking wheels against rails was loud and sharp in the air as the train ground to a halt. Ki disengaged the drive wheels and ducked reflexively as a bullet from somewhere whipped past his head and spanked off the iron plate before him, smashing one of the steam gauges.

A strange, almost melancholy roar began from beyond the tracks, and Ki lifted his head cautiously to see what was happening there.

They were coming. The witches had appeared from out of the woods, and with rifles in their hands, with a weird keening filling their mouths, they approached the train. They came on slowly, taking an occasional shot but remaining erect, moving at an almost casual pace.

"What in God's name is the matter with them?" Roger Travis asked. "Do they think they're immortal?"

"I think they wish to die," Ki answered. "I think they want to return to what they believe is their home."

One of them did as a bullet from somewhere on the knoll behind them tagged one of the witches in the breast and she slumped to the ground, dead.

"Ki!" Jessica said frantically, but he could only shake his head. He could do nothing to save these forlorn and bloodthirsty women. None of them could.

Roger Travis never could bring himself to fire a shot; nor could Jessie and Ki raise their weapons and shoot at the women who now attacked the train.

It made no difference—the Welsh and Chinese, the townspeople, perhaps in retaliation against past wrongs, opened up with withering fire, and they went down one by one, these sad lost things, and if there was a hell or a Dark Master, then they went home, all of them.

Ki suddenly saw the man he wanted.

Manning, exhorting his witches on and then seeing them fall one by one, had showed himself briefly before turning back to the forest, heeling his horse into a run.

"I'm taking your horse," Ki said to a surprised Roger Travis. The army bay was the nearest animal. Perhaps its battle time had inured it to the roar of gunfire all around, but whether that was so or not, it stood nearby, quivering yet motionless.

Ki hit the saddle on a run and yanked the horse's head around, leaning low across the withers as he raced after the fleeing Manning.

A gunhand loomed up from behind a fallen tree and aimed a chance shot at Ki. Fortunately he missed. Ki hadn't even seen the man. His whole attention was on the fleeing figure of Manning, who was now into deep timber, spurring his horse upslope.

There was more gunfire behind him and smoke still

177

streamed into the sky, but Ki was oblivious to all of this. He wanted Manning, wanted him so badly that his stomach knotted up as he thought of the man who had caused all of this death and destruction. Manning had used his own daughter and a group of young, disaffected girls to further his mad schemes. Never considering what he was doing to human beings, he had built a shabby, dark empire on their bodies.

Ki caught a glimpse of the pale horse Manning rode, had a fleeting image of the dark, caped figure riding it impressed on his eye as he topped the ridge.

Ki turned his mount sharply to the right and bore down on the fleeing Manning. His entire body was rigid, fired with an anger and vengeance he hadn't felt for a long while. This was an evil thing he pursued, not a man, but a savage creation of his dark lord.

He was heading toward the cliffs, it seemed, and his caves along the river. Why, Ki could only guess.

Ki urged his horse on faster. He saw the dark object in Manning's hand lift and saw the muzzle flash as the warlock fired across his shoulder at Ki, who ducked out of instinct, though the shot was far wide and to the left.

Manning was in timber again, and Ki leaned far forward across his horse's neck, straining to keep him in sight.

The crimson lining of his cloak gave Manning away. It fluttered like a red flag as Manning rode on in panic. Ki set his jaw and rode on.

By the time he reached the bluffs, Manning was already on his way down the trail. Ki didn't hesitate. Dismounting on the run, he hurled himself into space, hitting Manning squarely on the shoulder with one foot.

The horse reared up sharply, and both men started a long tumbling roll downslope toward the riverbed below. They landed, Manning on top of Ki, with enough force to drive the wind from both of them. Manning was on his feet first, the gun still miraculously in his hand.

The warlock grinned maliciously, his eyes lighting as he trained the gun's muzzle on Ki. Ki's leaping kick came as a violent shock to Manning. His expression was washed away by pain as Ki's heel slammed into his ribcage, knocking the pistol away as Manning's grip faltered.

Enraged, Manning bellowed a single word Ki couldn't comprehend, and holding his ribs, he started toward the river. Ki slipped just a little, and it was time enough to give Manning the lead he needed. He was into the river and being swept away by its current in a moment.

The last Kiai saw of him was the crimson of his cape floating on the swift surface of the river.

Ki wiped back his hair and muttered a savage curse as he ran for Manning's horse, standing, head down, at the foot of the trail.

Leaping onto the startled, still stunned animal's back, he set out at a gallop down the beach. The riverbank became narrower and rocky, forcing Ki to slow the horse. By then he had entirely lost sight of Manning, and there was no way of telling if the warlock had emerged on the far bank, drowned or was still being carried downstream.

Ki rode on for another mile, then crossed the river at a ford, doubling back to check the far bank for tracks, some sign that Manning had emerged from the water. But the gravel of the beach gave him no clue.

Reluctantly, his mood dark, he eventually turned the horse back toward the bluffs. His only hope was that Manning's body would wash up and be seen. If the man lived, more lives would be corrupted, more young women tortured, more men killed.

Back at the train, Jessica and the railroad men had taken the offensive.

The cowboys had withdrawn into the trees, many of them leaving their horses behind. Jessica, mounted now on one of these, moved cautiously through the trees, her eyes searching each shadow, awaiting the slightest sight or sound that did not belong in the forest.

To her left a rifle banged away twice, but whatever was taking place was out of her sight, cut off by a wooded knoll. She hadn't seen Travis for a while, but she knew approximately where he was—to her right and behind her, moving afoot through the trees. Farther north a picket line of lumbermen had formed itself, and they were moving slowly toward the ridge, combing the pines for the enemy.

The patch of color where none belonged brought the barrel of Jessica's rifle around sharply. The cowboy loomed up from out of nowhere, Colt in hand.

Jessie's shot was quicker. Firing across the saddlebow without taking real aim, her shot nevertheless went true. The cowboy reeled back, arms flailing like windmills, and he crumpled up against the grass to slowly bleed to death.

"Good shot," Jessica heard from behind her. Almost simultaneously she heard the ratcheting of a hammer being drawn back. She started to turn, but a sharp command halted her in mid-motion.

"I wouldn't do that, lady," Dan Fellows advised her. "I've got the drop on you, haven't I?" Then he said, "Drop the rifle."

Reluctantly Jessica opened her hands, and the Winchester fell softly to the grassy earth beneath her. Fellows came a little closer, his gun steady.

"What do you want?" Jessica asked.

"Just the horse, lady," Fellows said.

"Had enough of the fighting, have you?"

"Just about," Fellows admitted.

It was then that Roger Travis, moving softly, appeared

around the trunk of a big oak. Fellows, quicker to move, slammed his pistol against the side of the officer's head, and he went down to lie unconscious, his body involuntarily twitching.

Jessica made a growling sound in her throat and launched herself at Fellows. The big man managed to step back and trip her when she landed, and Jessica went sprawling on hands and knees beside the unconscious Travis.

She glared up at Fellows like a cat, her lip turned back savagely. "Go ahead, you've got the gun—shoot us both!" she shrieked.

Dan Fellows shook his head. "No, lady, I told you all I wanted was the horse. I don't like what I saw today—women dying all around me. I always rode for the brand, but this is one time I'm cutting my line free. I got to get going," he said as he glanced back to where the lumbermen and towns-people were approaching through the trees. He touched his hat brim and said, "I got to get going, lady. It's a long ride to Texas, and I mean to get there alive."

Then he swung aboard Jessie's horse and headed toward deeper timber.

Travis came slowly alert, his eyes still dazed. After another long minute he managed to get to his feet with Jessica's help.

The sheriff had appeared now, three men with him. He tipped back his hat and told Jessica, "It looks like it's pretty much over. Those that could, have run; those that couldn't, are either prisoners—or they're dead.

"Damned if I know what to do with all the prsioners, though," the lawman said. "My prison's kinda puny for the collection we got."

"We're taking them on the train with us through to Vas-quez," Roger Travis said decisively. "There are federal laws against some of what they've done. Interfering with govern-ment supply lines, for one."

181

Later, then, the captured cowboys were loaded onto one of the Pullmans, and guarded front and rear, they rode that way back to Collins.

"We'll not lose much time," Jessica explained to the sheriff. "And that way we can drop you and the townspeople off, take on a few supplies and head back for the head of the tracks."

"And Rebecca," Ki put in.

"Yes. I don't want to leave her behind. Especially not if there's a chance, as Ki says, that somewhere out there Manning is still roaming free. He'd be sure to come after his daughter again."

Roger Travis added, "She'll be safe enough on the army post. The officers' wives will take her in until she decides what she wants to do."

The train backed up the tracks then to Collins, moving through the timberlands with its load of prisoners, somber and glaring men.

The town was rebuilding, but it still looked dismal after the fire. It wasn't cheerful, with its rutted streets and blackened buildings, but there was enough cheer in it to satisfy Kiai as he stepped down from the train to the platform and caught sight of Rebecca Manning scurrying toward him, her skirt held up, her eyes alight.

Chapter 22

The skies were clear as the train steamed on toward Fort Vasquez, nearing the completion of its journey. The army post itself was near enough to be seen beyond a last stand of trees.

"What about the cattle?" Ki asked Jessica.

"Someone will have to make a decision on that. I'd favor selling them and turning the money over to whatever relatives Carl Dantley has left behind."

Dantley's body had been found. The cattleman had lost his big gamble. "Travis will talk to the colonel, and I suppose he'll have to get a clarification of what to do with the beef. Perhaps from Washington."

Travis had gone ahead to the fort with Rebecca. Later he had returned to the train with a contingent of troopers to lead the prisoners to the stockade at Vasquez.

"She looks fine, doesn't she?" Ki asked wistfully, looking toward the fort.

"Rebecca? She looks real fine, Ki." Jessica touched his shoulder. "Go on ahead if you want to."

The army had decided the train should make its last triumphal mile in style. Dignitaries, military and civilian, would be waiting for its arrival in top hats or dress uniform. A brass band would play, and no doubt there would be several speeches, all too long.

The colonel would ride in the locomotive with Jessica Starbuck and be allowed the doubtful privilege of blowing the whistle as the train came down the final grade.

"I'll wait," Ki said. "Perhaps she needs some time to be around the womenfolk, to pretty up and do shopping. No, I've come this far with this clanking monstrous thing; I'll see the last mile."

In the morning the small contingent from the fort arrived, pressed and polished. The colonel, a tall, spare man with a clipped gray mustache, was shown the train and introduced around before he glanced at his gold watch and announced his readiness. He was led ceremoniously to the locomotive, the nose of which was decorated with red, white and blue bunting. Jessica, in a green dress, was helped aboard, and Ki clambered up after her.

The engineer, wearing a new set of gray and white striped coveralls and matching cap, engaged the gears, and the train lurched twice before moving down the long grade toward the waiting town.

The train made its own breeze of about twenty miles an hour as it gained momentum and sailed down the iron rails toward Vasquez. The colonel, trying hard to look dignified, nevertheless had a boyish, happy expression on his face as the engineer rolled the train toward the fort and the waiting celebration.

Ki was enjoying the ride, even after all those days aboard. The feeling was one of both satisfaction and relief. The job was done.

Jessica rested a hand briefly on his shoulder and he smiled at her.

Fort Vasquez was ahead, and Rebecca, awaiting his embrace.

The pines seemed to whistle past now as the locomotive rolled on, seemingly with new energy. The colonel looked

184

toward the low, flat military post and the surrounding jumble of buildings, and his hand involuntarily stretched toward the whistle cord suspended above it.

"Now, do you think?" he asked Jessica Starbuck stiffly. Still his cheeks were flushed with the eagerness of a boy with a marvelous new toy.

"Whenever the notion strikes you," Jessie answered with a smile.

The whistle tooted once experimentally and then twice more, steam escaping into the cool Colorado air with each voicing.

"Son of a bitch!"

It was the engineer who suddenly blurted this out, and Jessica saw him grab frantically for the brake handle. The colonel began to toot the whistle more seriously. It blared out at the empty day.

It was a moment more before Jessica saw what was happening. The train was rolling along smoothly, and in the distance she could see sunlight gleaming on the instruments of the brass band, see people craning their necks on the newly built platform as the locomotive drew near.

Then she saw *him*.

Standing on the tracks ahead of them was a man with arms upraised, eyes lost in his face like black holes in his skull. The wind twisted his tattered cape around him as he waited for the onrushing train.

"What in God's name is he doing?" the colonel shouted as the train rumbled on downslope toward the expectant town. "He's mad!"

The colonel hung on the whistle cord now as Manning, his movements inexplicable, stood his ground. Yes, Jessica could have told the army officer, he is mad. He had always been mad, and now, with his war lost, he was determined to stop the train that had consumed his wild thoughts for so long.

"The Dark Master," Jessica said, but only Ki heard her, and only he would have known what she meant. Manning continued to serve his Dark Master, and he expected the power of his underworld lord to come upon him. He expected to stop the train with incantations and main power.

"Jesus, God!" the colonel shouted. "Will you stop the train or won't you?"

But there was no stopping the solid rush of the driving locomotive wheels, no stopping Manning from believing what he wished. The brakeman's efforts were as futile as the colonel's constant steam whistle.

"I don't want to see it," Jessica said. The warlock, his arms wildly waving, still stood his ground, as the train closed in.

Ki didn't want to see it either, but he did. The man in the scarlet and black cape, still waving his arms, did a little crazed jig step and then disappeared under the locomotive, making no more sound or impact than an insect would have.

Jessie stepped nearer to Ki, and he looped an arm around her shoulders, feeling her shudder a little as the train rolled into Fort Vasquez, brass band blaring, whistle still shrieking. There, dignitaries applauded delicately, and the colonel, visibly shaken, stepped down to the platform to run through the formal ceremonies.

Ki stepped down to find Rebecca waiting. She was there, and Roger Travis in a new uniform, sporting new captain's bars on his epaulets. In a group of four they walked to the presentation platform as the band played on.

None of them looked back up the tracks to where the dark, twisted figure lay.

He had finally met his Dark Master.

Watch for

LONE STAR AND THE BOUNTY HUNTERS

97th novel in the exciting LONE STAR series
from JOVE

Coming in September!